I0534211

Never Stop Skating

Other books by Jesse A. Murray

Love or Baseball?

I Will Never Break

Never Found

Not Here To Stay

Back Home

Falls Into Place

The Lucky Purple Sock

Never Stop Skating

A Novel

Jesse A. Murray

Off the Field Publishing
2024

Off the Field
Publishing

Copyright © 2024 by Jesse A. Murray

First Paperback Edition Published 2024

All rights reserved. This book or any portion thereof may not be reproduced or used in any manner whatsoever without the express written permission of the publisher except for the use of brief quotations in a book review or scholarly journal.

First Printing: 2024

Paperback ISBN: 978-1-7775913-4-2

eBook ISBN: 978-1-7775913-5-9

Off the Field Publishing
Saskatoon, Saskatchewan, Canada

Off the Field
Publishing

Book design by Jesse A. Murray
Cover image: © Jesse A. Murray

This book is a work of fiction. Any reference to historical events, real companies, real people, or real places are used to make this completely made up story, a more believable experience for the reader. Other names, characters, places, and events are products of the author's imagination, and any resemblance to actual events or places or persons, living or dead, is entirely coincidental.

For my nephew, Ryder.
Never stop skating.

Never Stop Skating

—PART 1—

GRADE SIX

CHAPTER 1

Every boy in Jay Noble's new neighbourhood played hockey. During that first winter in Saskatoon, Jay noticed that there were kids on the rink outside his frosted bedroom window, from right after school until late at night. It didn't matter if it was forty below zero outside, they would be out there.

After school, Jay would stand on his bed and watch the other kids skate around and glide on the rink. It looked so effortless. So many people would come together, and every time someone stepped on the ice, it looked like it brought so much joy. In between the noise of the slapping of sticks, and pucks bouncing off the posts and boards, Jay could often hear laughter.

On November 27th—exactly three days after his eleventh birthday—Jay stood on his bed again, and wished he could be out there skating with the other kids.

He had never played hockey before. Jay had only skated a few times when he was four or five years old, but that was when his dad still lived with him and his mom. That was around six years ago and he had long outgrown those barely used skates, but those were the only skates he ever owned.

Jay and his mom moved to Saskatoon in early August, so his mom could go back to school to become a lawyer. They now lived with his grandma and grandpa in the house that his mom grew up in. It wasn't the biggest house on the street, but it backed a school park, and in that park, he could see the school's outdoor hockey rink from his bedroom window.

Jay's breath started to create a large frost patch on his

window. He then glided his fingernail through the patch of frost, as if his finger was gliding on a rink.

He began to make another rink on the window with his hot breath, when his mom's voice broke his concentration.

"Jay," his mom said from his doorway. "Your grandma wants to know if you want to help her bake some gingersnap cookies."

He loved his grandma's gingersnap cookies. He used to love it when his grandparents came to visit him and his mom in Calgary, because they always brought gifts for him—including cookies.

"I guess," he replied turning away from the window to look at his mom. He didn't know if he actually wanted to help make his favourite cookies. He only wanted to eat the end result.

She walked over to him, and looked at the scratched-up frost patches on the window. "You watching the other kids play hockey again?"

"Could I get a pair of skates, mom?" he said not answering her question, and hopped down from his bed.

"We'll see, honey. I don't have any extra money right now, but maybe next month," she said as she moved her hand through Jay's soft, sandy brown hair.

Jay and his mom had the same colour of hair, and they both had light brown eyes that sparkled when they smiled.

Jay ducked away from his mom's hand, and moved toward his bedroom door. "Could grandma and grandpa buy me some?"

His mom followed him to the door. "Oh, Jay...grandma and grandpa don't have a lot of money either right now. It wasn't easy for them to help us move back here. Maybe we can ask them if they have kept any of your uncle's old skates that you could use."

Jay forgot all about helping his grandma bake cookies, and he ran down the stairs.

CHAPTER 2

"Hi, grandma, do you know where grandpa is?" Jay said as he slid into the kitchen.

"Jay Easton Noble! What did I say about running in the house? You almost flew through the refrigerator!" Jay's grandma said.

Jay's grandma didn't seem like a grandma. She looked a lot younger than other kid's grandmas, and was fit and athletic. She would often pretend to be mean, but she was really funny.

"Sorry, grandma," Jay said with a sheepish grin.

"He's outside salting the sidewalks," his grandma said. Before she could ask Jay if he was going to help her make cookies, Jay bolted toward the front door. "You better not be going outside wearing that," she tried to yell after him, but it was too late.

"Hey, grandpa!" Jay yelled as he ran down the ice-covered driveway wearing only shorts, a t-shirt, and some big, floppy sandals that he found in the front closet.

Why was Jay dressed for summer? Well, since he moved into his grandma and grandpa's house, it was always a lot warmer than what he was used to, so he would change into shorts and a t-shirt as soon as he got home from school. As for the sandals, he grabbed those because his boots were by the back door, and he didn't want to waste any time.

His grandpa stopped shaking the jug of sidewalk salt he was holding, and turned from the end of the driveway. He then took one look at his grandson, got a serious look on his face, was about to yell at him, but then changed his mind. He couldn't help but laugh. "Jay!" his grandpa said. "What do you think you're doing out here? Did you forget your towel? Are you headed to the beach?"

Jay's grandpa also didn't seem like a grandpa. He often wore a baseball cap and a hoodie and this made him look like a big kid. He could get angry sometimes, but he mostly cheered people up.

"No, grandpa, I want to go skating," Jay said proudly. He stood there with his hands on his hips in the minus twenty degrees Celsius weather. The cold didn't seem to bother him at all, and with the way he was standing, he looked like some strange superhero.

"Skating? You can't go skating dressed like that!" his grandpa shouted.

It was Jay's turn to laugh. "I know that. But I also can't go because I don't have any skates. My mom told me to ask if you have any of Uncle Dylan's old skates that I could try."

"I think we might. But let's go inside before you turn into a popsicle, and we can go look for them in the basement," Jay's grandpa said as he reached down and picked up an ice chipper with his free hand, and walked toward the house.

Jay took off running towards the front door, but his right sandal slid off and went into a snow bank.

Jay's grandpa shook his head as he watched his grandson hobble on one foot, step in the snow bank, grab his sandal, and run with one bare foot back into the house.

CHAPTER 3

Jay thumped down the basement stairs as quick as he could. He only went down there to watch TV sometimes with his grandpa, but now he was on a mission to find some hockey skates. He didn't know where to look, so he had to wait.

His grandpa came down—after what seemed like forever—and slid open a dark brown door near the basement bathroom. The door led to the furnace room, and Jay didn't even know that room existed. After his grandpa flicked on the light, Jay took a look around and saw a furnace, water heater, a large freezer, and two walls of shelves from floor to ceiling filled with stuff. It was dark, damp, and dusty. For some reason, he felt like he was searching for treasure. And in a way, he was.

"All the old sports equipment should be somewhere on these three shelves," Jay's grandpa said pointing to a mixture of cardboard boxes and blue plastic storage bins. "Your grandma always said she was going to go through everything and label them properly, but no such luck…we'll just have to start digging."

Jay opened the first dust covered blue bin, and immediately marveled at all of the things he found in there. He searched through a pile of old baseball and football equipment. There were jerseys, cleats, ball gloves, baseballs, and flattened footballs. Jay picked up everything and examined them with a mixture of curiosity and amazement. Jay didn't have much experience using any of this stuff except for a little at school. He always wanted to play sports, but back in Calgary his mom was always working, and was never able to sign him up for any teams.

"Bingo," his grandpa said as he opened a blue bin that he brought down from the top shelf.

Jay dropped an old catcher's mask back in the bin he was searching through, and headed over to his grandpa.

"Jackpot," Jay said looking in a bin full of skates, skates, and more skates.

The skates they found first were much too big, and were the ones his uncle wore in his last year of minor hockey.

"Look at the toe," his grandpa said handing a big skate to Jay, "your uncle was never afraid to block shots."

Jay looked at the toe, and saw a big crack in the plastic. "Whoa," he said. He couldn't imagine how hard a puck would have to hit to do that.

"I don't know why we kept a lot of this stuff…those skates won't be able to be used again," his grandpa said.

Those skates wouldn't be able to be used again, but Jay thought they were cool.

"What size of shoe do you wear? Skates usually fit one to two sizes smaller than your shoe size," his grandpa said as he matched two skates together, and put them flat on the concrete floor.

"I wear a size four shoe." Jay had just turned eleven, and he was smaller for his age. It never bothered him—until he moved to Saskatoon.

"You will need a size two or three skate," his grandpa said as he sorted through more skates. "If I remember, this could be tricky. Your uncle Dylan grew like a weed when he was around your age, and he jumped two skate sizes one season."

Jay hoped they could find something that would work. The further they dug, the smaller the skates were. His grandpa continued to sort through sizes, and matched up skates with Jay's help.

Jay's grandpa narrowed the search down to two pairs of skates. "Unfortunately, little buddy, looks like I was right. We have a pair of size twos," he said holding up a pair of old-looking

Bauer hockey skates, "and a pair of size fours," he said holding up a pair of newer-looking, but more beat-up CCM hockey skates. "Let's go out to the couch and try them on," he said as they left the furnace room, and out to the area where the couch and TV were.

Jay sat down on the black leather couch, while his grandpa loosened the laces on the smaller pair of skates, and handed them to him. "Try to put these on."

Jay shoved his right foot into one of the skates.

"Now try to slide your foot all the way forward," his grandpa said.

Jay tried to push forward, but there wasn't any room. They were narrow and snug.

"All right, let's get the other one on," his grandpa said, and handed Jay the second skate.

Jay put on the left skate, and didn't know what to do next.

His grandpa read his mind. "Know how to tie them?"

"Nope," Jay said shaking his head.

His grandpa knelt in front of Jay and grabbed his right skate. "Let me show you."

Jay's grandpa showed him how to tie skates properly. It was different than how he tied his shoes. His grandpa started near the toe and grabbed a loop in each hand and pulled. He continued this process until he reached the top, asking if that felt okay after each pull. Once he reached the top, he tied it like any regular shoe.

"There, you can stand up," his grandpa said.

Jay stood up, he started to fall over, and he had to grab his grandpa's arm for balance. "Go slow and try to walk a few steps," his grandpa reassured him.

Jay walked around on the soft basement carpet. He thought that if his grandma or mom saw what he was doing, he would have been in so much trouble. But his grandpa was the one telling him to do it, so it must have been fine.

Jay sat back down on the couch, and he loosened the skates

by doing the opposite of what his grandpa showed him.

He took off the size two skates, and put on the size fours.

His grandpa told him to push his foot all the way forward, and this time they had room to slide. They definitely were not as snug as the other pair.

"There is a lot more room in these ones," his grandpa said.

This time Jay tied his skates himself as tightly as he could. Jay stood up and his skates wobbled at the ankle. Jay tried to take a few steps, but he could tell they were too big.

"You'll grow into those soon enough, but I think you should try using the twos first," his grandpa suggested.

Jay agreed and he plopped back down on the couch, and untied the skates.

Before they went upstairs, Jay helped his grandpa put everything away in the storage room. When they were done, Jay charged up the stairs carrying both pairs of skates.

"Jay, stop!" Jay's grandpa yelled after him. Jay stopped midway up the stairs, and looked back at his grandpa. "Hasn't anyone ever told you to not run with scissors?"

Jay laughed. "Maybe."

"Well, the same goes with skates. Especially running on stairs holding four of them."

"Sorry, grandpa," Jay said and laughed again. "I'm just excited."

"That's fine. But be careful...I'll meet you up there."

Jay wanted to try his new skates as soon as possible, but he knew there were too many people out on the rink. He didn't want anyone to see him try to skate for the first time since he was a little kid—especially anyone from his school.

Jay went straight to the kitchen and found his mom and grandma doing the dishes. His grandma was washing and his mom was drying. Instantly, the smell of cookies baking in the oven hit him and his mouth started to water.

"Mom, do you think it would be all right if I woke up early

and went to the rink to skate tomorrow morning?" Jay asked.

"I'm sure your grandpa would be happy to take you out there right now if you asked him nicely," his mom said to Jay as she dried a mixing bowl with a white and blue dish towel.

"I don't know if I can even skate. The other kids will make fun of me if they see me out there."

Jay's mom looked at him concerned. "They wouldn't make fun of you, Jay-Jay."

Jay thought about telling her that the other boys already wouldn't let him play hockey with them at recess, and that wasn't even with skates on, but he decided not to.

"I just want to learn on my own. Okay, mom?"

"Well, okay. What time are you planning to get up?" his mom said. She opened a cupboard, and put the mixing bowl inside.

"Can I go out there at six thirty in the morning, and skate for an hour, and come back and get ready for school?" Jay asked.

"Let me get this straight," his mom said looking amused. "You are asking me if you can get up before six thirty in the morning?"

"Yeah. What's the big deal?"

"What's the big deal? Let me tell you what the big deal is," his mom said. "Do you not remember when I had to come in your room on four separate occasions this morning to get you up for school? And when you finally got out of bed, you were moaning and walking around like a mummy that just woke up from five thousand years of sleep."

Jay laughed. "I wasn't that bad. But can I at least try to wake up early tomorrow?

"That's so early, but you can give it a try. If you feel too tired when you wake up, you can go back to bed. How does that sound?"

"Sounds good. Thanks, mom!" Jay said. He knew that there was no way he would be too tired—6:30 a.m. couldn't come soon enough.

The timer went off on the oven, which meant the cookies were done. Jay got two pairs of skates, and now his grandma's gingersnap cookies. *Can this night get any better?* he thought.

After Jay and his grandpa ate more cookies than his mom and grandma would have liked, Jay took both pairs of skates to his room. He decided that he would try the ones that were too small the next day, and he put the other ones under his bed. If he could squeeze his feet in, that's all that mattered to him. Besides, nothing could hurt more than the pain of not having any friends at his new school because he couldn't play hockey.

That night, he could barely get to sleep he was so excited. He put a towel underneath his bedroom door to block the light—so no one knew he was up—and he practiced tying and untying his skates.

He tied them up one last time and stood up on his bedroom carpet. He pretended that he was on the ice, and imagined that one day, he would be the fastest skater that ever lived.

CHAPTER 4

Jay's alarm went off at 6:03 a.m.—he always set his alarm with a three in the minutes because that was his favourite number—and he popped out of bed excited for the day.

On any other regular school day, he never wanted to get out of bed to go to school. His mom often had to try to wake him up several times, and he would moan and groan. Eventually she would have to pull all the covers off. Sometimes that wouldn't even work

Jay grabbed his sweats and snow pants that he set out the night before, and put them on. He was more ready for this day than any other day since he moved to Saskatoon.

As he dressed, he could hear his grandpa in the kitchen making coffee. Jay's eyes felt a bit tired, but the rest of him was full of energy.

Jay picked up his skates from beside his bed, opened his bedroom door, and headed downstairs to the kitchen. As he was going to say "Good morning" to his grandpa, he saw a wooden hockey stick leaning up against the counter. He immediately went over to check it out.

"Grandpa, is this mine?" he said putting the skates down on the counter beside the sink.

"Good morning to you too, Jay," his grandpa said with a smile. He didn't realize it quite yet, but having his grandson living with him gave him more energy than he had in a long time. "I found it in the garage. It was your uncle Dylan's, but I cut it down, and taped it for you. Every hockey player needs a hockey stick.

So, it's all yours now."

"Thanks, grandpa!"

"You're welcome, little buddy. Now, before we head out, you have to eat some breakfast."

"Do I have to?" Jay asked as he examined the fresh black tape on the blade of his new stick.

"Of course you do. You need breakfast to give you energy to skate. It's the most important meal of the day."

Jay had heard that before, but he still never liked breakfast.

"So, what will it be? Toast? Cereal? Brown sugar with a little bit of oatmeal?" his grandpa asked.

His grandpa liked to tease him when Jay ate oatmeal. Jay would put in so much brown sugar, and his grandpa would say that he was eating a bowl of brown sugar with a little bit of oatmeal mixed in. But that's the only way Jay would eat it.

Jay laughed. "I'll take the bowl of brown sugar, please."

Jay's grandpa filled the kettle in the sink, and put it on the stove. "Coming right up."

His grandpa continued to make Jay's oatmeal, while Jay pretended to stickhandle an imaginary puck on the kitchen floor.

"Don't let your grandma see you do that," his grandpa warned.

"Don't let me see what?" his grandma said entering the kitchen. "Jay Easton Noble! No playing hockey in my kitchen!"

"Sorry, grandma," Jay said. "I just can't wait to use my new stick!"

Jay's grandma smiled. She probably would have grounded any of her kids for a week for playing hockey in the kitchen, and another week for putting skates on the counter. But being a grandma was different. For some reason she would let her beautiful grandson get away with anything. "Pass me the puck," she said holding an imaginary stick.

Jay passed her the imaginary puck. She shot the imaginary puck toward the oven and raised her arms in the air. "She shoots, she scores!" his grandma announced.

"What is going on in here?" Jay's mom said with a yawn as she walked in.

"Grandma scored the game winning goal," Jay said as he leaned on his hockey stick.

"You are all nuts…it's just after six in the morning. I should not have let you get up this early, kiddo," she said rubbing her hand over Jay's hair. "Any coffee left, dad?"

"There's still half a pot. But make sure there is a little left for me to top up my mug to take to the rink with me," Jay's grandpa said.

They all took a seat at the table and watched Jay shovel his oatmeal into his mouth. He looked like some sort of wild beast, and he was making strange noises while he wolfed down his food.

"Umm, Kiddo?" his mom said.

Jay looked up from his bowl. "Yeah?"

"Slow down. You're scaring us," his mom said.

Jay snorted. "Sorry, mom."

He went back to finishing his breakfast—and he tried to eat a bit slower after that.

When he finished—in almost world-record-setting time—he swiftly rinsed out his bowl, and put it in the sink. Then, he grabbed his stick, and ran to put on his winter jacket, gloves, and tuque. Everything he did that morning was at top speed.

Before they left, his grandpa handed him his skates. "Don't forget these," his grandpa said.

"Thanks, grandpa," Jay replied taking the skates and putting them down beside his boots.

"Have fun, kiddo," Jay's mom called out.

"Score some goals," his grandma added.

Jay and his grandpa put on their winter boots, grabbed their stuff, and headed out the back door. As soon as Jay stepped outside, he couldn't believe how dark it was. It felt like it was the middle of the night, and the whole world was asleep.

They walked through the backyard, opened the gate, and trekked across the snow-covered field to the hockey rink. There was already a small, packed-down path where Jay had been walking to and from school each day, for the last three weeks since it first snowed. As the snow crunched under his boots with each step, Jay noticed the bright moon was shinning off the white snow, and he thought it was magical. He was about to start a new adventure.

When they got to the rink, Jay put on his skates. They felt even tighter that morning, but he stuffed his feet in, and didn't say anything to his grandpa. Then he tied his skates just like his grandpa showed him the night before.

When he was done, his grandpa handed him his stick, and Jay clumsily walked through the snow until he got to the ice. The second he stepped on the ice, one skate went forward, and the other one went backward, and he fell hard on the ice.

Jay's grandpa rushed over. "Are you all right, little buddy?" his grandpa asked.

"I'm fine," Jay said, and he crawled over to the boards, and slowly pulled himself up. He had a memory of his dad holding him up by the shoulders, and letting him go when he was ready. But he mostly walked on the ice with skates on back then. Now he wanted to actually skate.

"Take it nice and easy," his grandpa said. "Bend your knees and find your balance, and then you can start moving."

Jay took a deep breath, bent his knees, found his balance, and leaned on his stick in front of him. He carefully pushed off with his right skate, and then his left skate, and glided by leaning and balancing on this stick. "Good," his grandpa hollered. "Now keep doing that."

Jay pushed with his right skate, then left, then glided. He did that a few times, and then made his way back to where his grandpa was standing.

"You are doing great. But look at me. You are still pushing

off like you are running. For skating, you want to turn the toe of your skate outward a bit, and dig in with your blades to take a more powerful stride. That's how you pick up speed. Just like this." His grandpa showed Jay what a proper stride would look like with his big, white winter boots.

Jay nodded his head, and tried himself. He was able to dig in more, but it still wasn't perfect. He needed to work on his balance. He continued to take strides around the rink, but he was leaning heavily on his stick.

As he got more comfortable, he tried to go faster and faster, but he didn't know how to stop. He fell and crashed into the boards many times, but he always got right back up and started skating again.

Meanwhile, his grandpa drank coffee, shouted out some words of encouragement, and watched his grandson have the time of his life.

After almost an hour, his grandpa called him in. "Jay! It's time to go get ready for school."

Jay was having so much fun and he didn't want to stop skating. "A couple more laps, grandpa?"

"A couple more and that's it. Make them quick."

Jay dug in, and tried to skate as fast as he could possibly go—which wasn't very fast. But with the cold wind blowing on his numb face, he felt like he was flying around the rink. As he was finishing his second lap, and since he still didn't know how to stop, he decided to dive forward like a baseball player diving into home plate. The snow sprayed up into his face as he slid, and he came to a stop right by where his grandpa was standing.

"Safe!" his grandpa announced and held out his arms like an umpire.

Jay laughed, then put his head down and pretended to sleep right there on the ice.

"Got to get up, little buddy."

"Do I have to?" Jay moaned.

"I'm afraid so," Jay's grandpa said. Jay got up to his knees and he was covered in snow from head to toe. "Let's go, Mr. Snowman," his grandpa added.

Jay laughed, got up to his skates, and made his way off the ice. Jay wasn't discouraged about his morning practice. He knew skating wasn't going to be easy, but he was surprised at how fast he could go. Once he learned stopping, and turning, he knew he would be much better.

When he got off the ice, he felt like a different kid. He felt like he found what he was meant to do. He walked back to his house with his grandpa and couldn't wait to skate again the next day.

Jay woke up early, and skated while most kids were sleeping, and he didn't feel tired at all. He thought it was one of the best things he had ever done, and he wanted to keep doing it.

That day, he was also excited to bring his hockey stick to school and play hockey with the rest of the boys at recess. Jay was filled with hope. Maybe he would finally have some friends. Maybe he would eventually be out there playing hockey with them on the outdoor rink after school. Maybe, moving to Saskatoon wasn't so bad after all.

CHAPTER 5

Jay carried his hockey stick proudly across the field, past the rink, and to the school. When he got to his classroom, he put his stick behind the door where all the others were kept.

From time to time, while he was supposed to be learning, he would look behind that door, and think how lucky he was to have his own hockey stick. Jay's stick was older, and it was made out of wood, but that didn't bother him. As long as he had something to play with, he was happy.

When the bell rang for that first recess, Jay followed all the other boys out to the back of the school. Nobody seemed to pay attention to him as he walked up and threw his stick in the pile with all the rest. One of the boys kneeled over the sticks with his black tuque over his eyes, and he began picking up sticks one by one and tossing them to opposite sides. This was the same method they used to pick teams each day. As the sticks were being tossed, all the boys watched with laser-like focus to see where theirs ended up.

Jay started to walk over to where his had been thrown, but a boy in his class named Brendan Walker—who was almost a foot taller than all the other boys—got to it before he did.

Brendan was the class clown, class bully, and the class cool kid all wrapped up into one.

"Whose is this piece of crap?" Brendan said as he picked up Jay's stick and held it up for all to see. "Is this even a hockey stick? Looks like something my grandpa would use."

"What is that, Gordie Howe's stick?" another boy named

Ryan Fitzgerald added.

A bunch of the boys laughed.

Brendan and Ryan were best friends, and they were always together. Ryan was small, but he was loud and had a big mouth.

Jay was so embarrassed when he saw that it was his stick. He was so happy when his grandpa gave it to him, and he was so proud to bring it to school so he could fit in, but that all vanished in a second. He didn't understand. Wasn't a hockey stick simply a hockey stick?

Jay didn't know what to do. Part of him wanted to walk away without saying anything. But a stronger part of him wanted to play hockey with his classmates, and hopefully make some friends.

He took a deep breath, claimed his stick, and added a lie. "That's mine," Jay said holding out his hand in front of Brendan. "And yeah, it is a piece of crap. I broke my good stick yesterday, and brought this one last minute. I think it was my uncle's or something."

"Noble, I didn't know you played hockey," Brendan said.

"I did before I moved here," Jay lied again.

"Let's see what you can do," Brendan said handing Jay his wooden stick.

Everyone automatically lined up for the face off, and Jay didn't know where to stand. But that didn't seem to matter. The game started with two boys slapping their sticks together over the tennis ball, and shouting "N, H, L" with each slap. On the last slap, they battled for the ball.

The game started, and Jay was playing recess hockey for the first time.

Jay instantly realized how good the boys were at hockey. They were playing with a tennis ball, and they were able to stickhandle around each other and shoot the ball harder than he could have imagined. He watched them play from a distance before, but as he was running around with them, he found out that he couldn't do the things they could do. However, he did notice that he didn't have to be good at stick handling when he was playing defense. Since he was faster than a lot of the other boys, he was able to knock the ball off the other team's sticks, and pass it to a teammate.

Brendan—who was on the other team—was the best player in the class. He was tall, quick, and could handle the ball unlike anyone else. But Jay was determined, and he was able to catch up to him, and take the ball away.

After Jay took the ball away from Brendan a few times, Brendan got frustrated, and smashed his stick down on Jay's wooden stick. Brendan's stick snapped in half. It was clearly Brendan's fault, but he blamed Jay.

"Look what you did. You broke my stick!" Brendan screamed.

"I did not! You broke your own stick," Jay said.

Brendan shoved Jay to the ground.

Jay got up, but the teacher on supervision, Mr. Hamilton, was already there before anything else could happen.

"What's going on here?" Mr. Hamilton asked.

"He broke my hockey stick, and owes me a new one," Brendan said, pointing at Jay.

"I did not. He broke his own stick over mine," Jay said quietly.

"He's a liar!" Brendan shouted.

"All right boys, that's enough," Mr. Hamilton said. "We will go inside, and straighten all this out in the principal's office."

Jay's heart sank. He had never been in trouble before, and now he was in trouble for something he didn't do.

Mr. Hamilton took the boys inside, and brought them to their classroom. He explained to Miss Wallace—their grade six teacher—what he saw, and what each of the boys said. Miss Wallace looked at the boys, but Jay could have sworn that she looked mostly at him. She then gave a dirty look, and shook her head. It was as if they had just ruined her day, and now she had to do more work than she wanted to do.

Miss Wallace was unlike any other teacher Jay had back in Calgary. She was in her mid-forties, she was tall, a little heavier-set, had dark hair, dark eyes, and crooked teeth. He had strict teachers before, but she was different. She was a bully. Jay noticed that she would take the side of the popular girls and boys in the class, and sometimes she would join in when they would pick on other kids.

In class, one of her favourite things to do was to single students out, in order to make the other kids laugh. For example, she loved to catch someone daydreaming. She would say things like, "Earth to Melanie. Are you in class right now, or on the moon?" and the student's face would turn red from embarrassment, and the rest of the class would laugh at them. Or she always asked students that struggled with math, to answer questions on the board in front of everyone. Then, when they got it wrong, she would put a large red "X" through it and say, "Wrong again," to more snickers from the class. Jay thought she was awful, and he never laughed with the others.

"So let me get this straight, Brendan," she said as she put a stack of books down on her desk, "Jay slashed and broke your stick, and then he pushed you down?"

"That's exactly what happened," Brendan said.

Jay couldn't believe his ears. He couldn't believe that Brendan would lie like that.

"That's not what happened!" Jay said raising his voice for the first time to a teacher. "Brendan slashed and broke my stick, and then he pushed me down."

Miss Wallace's face turned red. "Jay, that's enough. I will not tolerate this bad behaviour and this lying."

"I'm not lying. Go ask the other teacher. You must have heard wrong," Jay said.

That made Miss Wallace even more angry. "I did not hear wrong. I know exactly what Mr. Hamilton told me," she said with clenched teeth and a scrunched-up face.

Obviously not, Jay wanted to say, but he knew he should be quiet. Her angry and scrunched-up face and her large crooked teeth scared Jay. He was new to the school that year, but now he knew why some of the other students called her "Miss Walrus" behind her back.

"Brendan, you can go sit at your desk and wait for everyone else to come back from recess," she said pointing at his desk. "Jay, we're going to the principal's office. And now we will have to call Brendan's parents to see how much his stick will cost to replace. Then we will have to call your mom to let her know what you did, and how much she will have to pay to replace Brendan's stick."

Jay's eyes filled with tears. He knew his mom was going to be so upset.

"Let's go," Miss Wallace said, yanking Jay's sleeve.

"What a baby," Jay heard Brendan say as they walked out of the classroom.

Jay walked down the hallway following his teacher. He was so angry, and so sad at the same time. He couldn't believe this was happening. Why wouldn't anyone listen to the truth?

CHAPTER 6

When they got to the main office, Miss Wallace walked him straight into Mrs. Clarke's office.

Mrs. Clarke was a short lady, with short, grey hair, and thin silver glasses. For some reason, to Jay, she didn't seem like a principal. Maybe it was because at his old school in Calgary, the principal was a large man, with a loud voice, and talked often about his days playing football in the CFL. Jay never got in trouble in Calgary, but that was a good thing, because his old principal was intimidating. Mrs. Clarke, on the other hand, looked like she was someone's great-grandmother.

Without any kind of greeting to the principal, and before Jay could tell his side of the story, Miss Wallace told Mrs. Clarke everything that happened at recess.

Mrs. Clarke looked at Jay and asked, "Is this true?"

Before he could answer, Miss Wallace spoke for him again. "Not only did Jay do all these things, but he was also lying about it which is even worse."

The bell rang to signal that recess was over.

"Thanks, Jeanie, you better get back to your class," Mrs. Clarke said to Jay's teacher. "I can take it from here."

Miss Wallace left, and Jay felt a bit of relief.

"Mr. Noble, you can come take a seat," Mrs. Clarke said.

Jay sat on a chair that the principal motioned towards. He still had tears in his eyes.

"Well, Jay. What do you have to say for yourself? I can see that you feel pretty bad about what you did, which is a start."

Jay looked at the principal, and then down at the ground. He saw a black ant frantically exploring a large crumb of some variety. In a feat of strength, the ant picked up the crumb, and started to carry it under the principal's desk.

"I didn't do anything," he said without looking up.

"Now, now, Jay. You should know that lying is not acceptable."

"I'm not lying. Go ask anyone that was playing hockey at recess. They will tell you what Brendan did."

"Jay, the teacher on supervision saw everything that happened. You just have to admit what you did, so we can figure out the consequences," Mrs. Clarke said.

Jay could feel the principal's eyes on him, but he didn't want to look up, and he didn't know what else to say. He felt so hopeless. Nobody would listen to him. He saw the ant again— without the crumb this time—and watched it scurry around the floor. Jay wondered if ants ever stopped moving.

"I'm going to go call Brendan's parents to find out how much the stick costs," Mrs. Clarke said as she got up from behind her desk. "I want you to think about what you did, and by the time I come back, I hope you are ready to admit it. Then we can talk about apologizing to Brendan."

Mrs. Clarke left her office, and Jay sat there looking at his laces. While he was alone, he started to get more angry than sad. He wondered how could Brendan be such a liar? And how could these adults so easily take Brendan's side? It wasn't fair.

But then he got sad again. Jay knew that there was no way that his mom would be able to afford a new stick for Brendan. It was only a week earlier, when Brendan was bragging about his brand-new composite stick that he brought for recess hockey. All the other kids marvelled at the new stick as they passed it to each other. Jay didn't know much about hockey, but he knew a stick like that was expensive.

Jay thought about how this incident would hurt his mom so

much. His mom couldn't afford skates and a stick for Jay, but now she would have to buy Brendan a new stick? Where would she get the money from? Would she have to get a job, and leave law school? Jay started to believe that him wanting to play hockey ruined everything for her. He decided that he wasn't going to play hockey ever again—even if he really wanted to. He thought that was the least he could do for his mom.

As he sat in the office feeling lost, he hoped that since Brendan seemed to have everything he wanted, maybe his parents wouldn't make Jay pay for the stick. That was Jay's only hope. But that hope didn't last.

The principal opened the door to her office, walked behind her desk, and sat down. "So, I spoke to Brendan's mom, and she said that the stick would cost two-hundred and fifty dollars to replace."

"Two-hundred and fifty dollars!" Jay blurted out.

"I must say that is a lot of money," she said as she swiveled her chair so she could look out of her office window. "When my boys played hockey, we would buy them sticks made out of wood that only cost around twenty dollars each…it sure is a different world out there."

Mrs. Clarke turned away from the window to face Jay again. Jay could see that his principal was upset, but he had the feeling it wasn't at him.

"I'm sorry, Jay," the principal continued. "But she expects the money within the next couple of days. So, I guess I will have to call your mom and let her know."

Jay felt defeated.

Twenty dollars was probably how much Jay's wooden stick cost. Yet, the two-hundred-and-fifty-dollar stick was the one that was broken. That didn't seem to make any sense.

The principal left the office once again, and Jay sat there wondering what he was going to do. Not long after the principal left, Jay's teacher flung the door open, dumped a pile of schoolwork on Jay's lap, and told him to get it done for tomorrow. Without any further explanation for what he needed to do, she then turned, walked out, and shut the door.

Jay sat there frozen holding on to the pile of work. He didn't have his binder, or even a pencil to write with.

The principal came in and out of her office throughout the morning, and Jay, not knowing exactly what he was supposed to do, pretended to read the textbooks and handouts that the teacher gave him. He was too upset to read. Too upset to do anything.

When the lunch bell rang, Jay sat in the office alone. Jay always walked home for lunch, but his teacher never came to check on him, and the principal didn't come back for the whole lunch break. Jay was too scared to leave. He sat in that office thinking about what his grandma would have made him for lunch. Would it be soup and sandwiches? Her homemade macaroni and cheese? Or maybe perogies? Jay's stomach grumbled. Lunch came and went, and the day felt like it was taking forever.

Finally, when the day was over, Jay was able to leave the principal's office and go grab his belongings from the classroom. When he got there, Miss Wallace was sitting at her desk. She didn't even look up as Jay started to pack his stuff up to go home.

"I forgot to give this to you," Miss Wallace said when Jay was about to leave.

Jay stopped and turned to look. She was holding up a brown paper bag. He didn't want to go back, but he rushed over and grabbed the bag from her. He was like a scared animal snatching a treat from someone's hand. She still didn't even look up.

As Jay walked to the classroom door, he opened the brown bag. Inside was a sandwich, three gingersnap cookies, carrot sticks, and a yogurt with a spoon. Someone had dropped off a lunch for him, and his teacher didn't even bring it to the principal's office. Jay couldn't believe she would punish him by making him go the whole day without a lunch. What kind of teacher was she?

Before he left the classroom, he went to grab his hockey stick and found that the blade was broken in half—it looked as if someone purposely stepped on it. There was no doubt in his mind that Brendan was the one responsible. Now he owed Brendan two-hundred and fifty dollars, and Jay didn't have a hockey stick for himself. The day was getting worse and worse, and he still had to go home and see the disappointment and stress on his mom's face.

The walk home was just across the field, but it was the most painful walk he ever had to make.

CHAPTER 7

Jay reached the gate to his grandma and grandpa's backyard and pulled the cord to unlatch the gate. He slowly walked through the backyard, and he heard a noise in the garage. He knew his grandpa was probably in there. He felt it was safest to tell him the real story, and to ask him how mad his mom was.

"Hi, grandpa," he said sheepishly as he entered the garage carrying his broken stick.

"Hey, little buddy," his grandpa said. "What happened to your stick?"

"My mom didn't tell you what happened today?"

"Oh, she told me. But I don't believe it for a second. I want to know what *really* happened."

"Grandpa, it was awful..."

Jay told him the whole story. The real story.

"Do you believe me, grandpa?" Jay said, catching his breath after he finished explaining everything.

"Of course, I do, little buddy," his grandpa replied. "We better go in and tell your mom what happened. She is very upset."

When Jay and his grandpa went into the house, his mom and grandma were drinking tea at the kitchen table. He saw the look on his mom's face and he felt terrible. He had seen that look before back in Calgary when she was working so much. It was the look of her being tired and overwhelmed.

"So, Jay, I heard you had quite the morning," his mom said, and she forced a small smile. "Can you tell me what happened?"

"I'm sorry, mom," he said, and her smile disappeared. She

was hoping that her son hadn't done what the school said. Jay went over to her and gave her a hug. He didn't hug her because he was feeling guilty, it was a hug that was meant to comfort her and make her feel better.

"Jay told me the whole story in the garage," Jay's grandpa said. "It sounds like he didn't do anything wrong. It's this other boy that did all those things that the school said Jay did."

"It's true, mom," Jay said. "I didn't do anything, honest. I didn't break his stick, and we shouldn't have to pay the two-hundred and fifty dollars…Brendan is the one that broke my stick. I found it after school with the blade snapped in half. I actually don't know if it was him for sure, but I'm guessing he did it. He always does stuff like that."

"What do you mean?" his mom asked.

Jay took a seat at the table, and focused on the fruit bowl centred in the middle. It was full of fresh apples and oranges.

Jay took a deep breath and started to explain. "Well, he picks on others a lot, but the teacher lets him get away with anything. He is always showing off, and brags about all the new things his parents buy him all the time. I don't know why, but everyone seems to like him."

Jay's mom thought about people she knew who were like that. They picked on others, and bragged, but were popular. It wasn't only kids, adults were like that, too.

"I will call the school and explain to the principal your side of the story," his mom said. She believed her son. He was always a sweet kid.

"Thanks, mom."

"Now go finish any homework before supper. We're having your favourite tonight," his mom said.

"All right, perogies!" Jay said. "I'll try and break my record since I never got to eat lunch."

"You'll turn into a perogy. And how will you skate if you are a perogy?" Jay's grandpa said to cheer his grandson up. "But what do you mean you didn't get to eat lunch? I dropped off some lunch for you."

The thought of being a perogy made Jay laugh. But he still wanted to try and eat seventeen perogies to break his record. "My teacher didn't give me the lunch you dropped off until after school," Jay said. "She told me she forgot to give it to me earlier."

"What? That is unacceptable. How do you forget to give a kid their lunch?" his grandma said. She was angry. She always made sure everyone was fed.

"I'll make sure I bring that up when I call the school tomorrow," Jay's mom added.

Jay went to his room and finished up some math homework that he wasn't able to focus on when he was in the principal's office. He hated math. To him, it was very boring, but at least he was good at it. He finished all his work promptly and moved on to reading a book.

Jay did like to read, however. When he moved to Saskatoon he found a box of hockey books in his uncle's old closet. Most of them were from the *Screech Owls Series* by Roy MacGregor. One night when Jay was bored, he dug out *The Night They Stole the Stanley Cup* from that box, and started to read. From then on, he became more interested in hockey. With the *Screech Owl Series*, he enjoyed the mysteries found in the stories, but most of all, he liked how it was about a hockey team. The more he read, the more he wanted to play hockey, and be on a team someday.

Just as the book started to get good, Jay's grandpa knocked on his bedroom door to tell him his pile of perogies were ready. Jay usually didn't eat anything else when he had perogies—that would only ruin his chances to break his record.

Jay was probably hungrier than he had ever been, but when he got to the kitchen, he knew this wouldn't be the night that he would be able to break his perogy-eating record. At his spot at the table was a bowl of borsht soup. Jay never used to eat borsht— that strange purple soup looked weird—but once he finally tried it, he loved it.

Jay knew he would eat at least two bowls of his grandma's homemade borsht—with almost half a pack of crackers crumbled in each bowl—and he would be too full to eat a lot of perogies. Jay also knew that his grandpa would make the comment, "Would you like some soup with those crackers?" just like he always did. It would be the same joke as the oatmeal and brown sugar from the morning, but would still make Jay laugh.

Jay grabbed the package of crackers, and was about to sit down when the doorbell rang several times. Only one person usually rang the doorbell that way, and Jay jumped up to go answer the door.

CHAPTER 8

"Hey, Uncle Dylan!" Jay said, as his uncle let himself in the front door.

Uncle Dylan was wearing a black winter jacket, and a grey tuque. His beard was looking a little longer than usual, and Jay thought it made him look even cooler. Jay couldn't wait until he could grow a beard like that.

Jay's uncle must have come straight from university. He was 22 years old and studying to get his Psychology degree—but he wanted to get into law school just like his older sister. For Jay, the best part of moving to Saskatoon, was that he got to see his favourite uncle a lot more often than before.

"Hey, Neph," Uncle Dylan said, and gave Jay a half-hug around his shoulder.

"Nobody told me you were coming over for supper," Jay said.

"It was a surprise visit," Uncle Dylan said. "Is that perogies and cabbage rolls I smell?"

"It sure is," Jay said, and walked with his uncle to the kitchen.

Jay and his uncle both didn't like cabbage rolls, but they sure loved perogies.

"You could always sniff out perogies across town, couldn't you?" Jay's grandpa said greeting his son.

"Come, sit," Jay's grandma ordered, as she set a plate for Uncle Dylan.

"Hey, Neph, are you going for your record tonight?" Uncle Dylan said as he grabbed a glass from the cupboard, and began to fill it with water at the sink.

Uncle Dylan was the one that introduced Jay to the idea of a perogy-eating record. Uncle Dylan said he once ate 33 and a half perogies, but felt like he was going to explode, and couldn't quite make it to 34. Jay's goal was to eat 33 someday, too.

"No, not today, Unc," Jay said. "Grandma made borsht,"

"Borsht and perogies…I did come on the perfect night," Uncle Dylan said, and then he took a long gulp of his water.

"What's with the beard, professor?" Jay's mom said to Uncle Dylan.

"Oh, this?" Uncle Dylan said rubbing his chin. "Isn't it beautiful?" he added while beaming a fake smile.

Uncle Dylan then walked over to the table, put his glass down, and sat at his spot beside Jay.

"I think you would look handsomer with a clean-shaven face," Jay's grandma said as she filled a bowl of soup for Uncle Dylan.

"So Jay and I could look the same age? I don't think so," Uncle Dylan said and chuckled. "Plus, this fur keeps me warm in the winter. It's freezing out there tonight."

"Speaking of freezing," Jay's grandpa said, "Jay used your old skates and your Koho hockey stick out on the rink this morning."

"Oh, the ol'Koho. I loved that stick. I scored a few goals with that one, hey, pop?" Uncle Dylan said.

"Yes, you did, Dyl, but unfortunately there was an incident at school today, and your *ol'Koho* got broken," Jay's grandpa said.

"What happened? Did you take a wicked slap shot, Neph? Top shelf?" Uncle Dylan asked.

Jay felt bad that he had been responsible for breaking his uncle's old stick the very first time he used it. "No, a kid at school stepped on it or something," Jay said as he crushed several crackers into his soup.

"There was one big misunderstanding at school," Jay's mom said.

"What kind of misunderstanding?" Uncle Dylan asked.

"Another kid broke his stick over mine, I mean, your stick, and then pushed me down, and told the teacher I did all those things," Jay told his uncle.

"And Jay had to spend the whole day in the principal's office, and they want me to pay two-hundred and fifty dollars to replace the other boy's hockey stick," Jay's mom said.

"You're not going to pay that, are you?" Uncle Dylan asked.

"No, I'm going to call the school tomorrow," Jay's mom replied.

"You know what I would have done if some other boy broke his stick over mine, pushed me, and blamed me?" Uncle Dylan said, and then he shoved a full perogy covered in sour cream into his mouth.

"Don't start!" his grandma warned Uncle Dylan.

"Jay's not you," Jay's mom said. "He's a sweet boy."

"What would you have done, Unc?" Jay asked. He wanted to know what his favourite uncle would have done.

"Let's just say this other boy would have a broken stick and a broken nose," Uncle Dylan said with a smirk.

"Hey, now! Don't give my boy any ideas. And things are different now. There is zero tolerance for fighting at schools nowadays," Jay's mom said.

"Brendan is a lot bigger than me anyway, it wouldn't be a good idea for me trying to fight him," Jay added.

"I beat up plenty of boys bigger than me, Neph. You just have to learn how to do it," Uncle Dylan said.

"Dylan!" Jay's grandma said, and gave him a look that all mothers can do.

"What? It's true, and you know it," Uncle Dylan said.

Jay's grandma frowned at Uncle Dylan, but didn't say anything else.

"Where did you learn how to fight?" Jay asked.

"Believe it or not, little man, your grandpa was quite the

fighter in his day, too. He's the one that taught me a few tricks," Uncle Dylan said.

"Grandpa, you were a fighter?" Jay asked.

"It was different times, Jay. But yes, I could hold my own," his grandpa said, as he dropped his fork, and flexed his bicep.

Jay's grandma and mom gave his grandpa a look of disappointment.

"Hmmph, boys," grandma said shaking her head.

"Boys, is right," Jay's mom added. "Let's change the subject."

Jay didn't want to change the subject. He had so many questions he wanted to ask. He couldn't imagine his grandpa being a fighter. He always seemed so friendly to everyone. But there was some part of Jay that wanted to learn how to defend himself. Maybe he could hold his own, too? Maybe he would be able to fight back if anyone tried to pick on him? At the same time, Jay never wanted to hurt anyone. It just wasn't him. But after that night, he thought more and more about wanting to learn how to fight. Maybe he could learn some tricks from his grandpa, just like his uncle did?

The conversation did move on to Uncle Dylan's university classes, and Jay lost interest. Jay finished his second bowl of borsht, and moved on to a plate of twelve perogies topped with sour cream. Jay didn't know if he could even eat that much after two bowls of soup, but he wanted to impress his uncle.

"Jay woke up at six this morning to go skate on the rink, so I'm sure you can get up for your classes," Jay's grandpa said to Uncle Dylan.

"Six in the morning! Why on earth would you do that, Neph?" Uncle Dylan asked.

"Because I want to learn how to skate when no one is out there," Jay replied.

"See, that's dedication. If your eleven-year-old nephew can get up that early to go skate before school, you can get up and go to your classes," Jay's grandpa said.

"Thanks, Neph. You're making me look bad over here," Uncle Dylan said jokingly.

Jay laughed. "Sorry, Unc."

"Dyl, maybe you can take Jay out sometime and teach him how to play hockey?" Jay's mom said.

"I would love to. Just not before school…deal?"

"Deal," Jay said. "Mom, am I allowed to go out again tomorrow morning, you know, after what happened today and all?"

"If you want to, Jay-Jay. I'm not going to let this bully at school take that away from you, too."

"Awesome!" Jay said.

"I still think you're crazy for wanting to go out there that early, Neph. But I can't wait to get out there with you one of these nights."

"I can't wait either," Jay said.

When they finished supper, Jay showed his uncle Dylan the skates he was using, and the old hockey books he had been reading. Uncle Dylan also showed Jay some simple moves that Jay could use if he ever got in a fight—he taught him how to swipe away a punch and counter with two quick punches. Uncle Dylan also told Jay all about his hockey days, and Jay got even more excited about learning how to play hockey. But before he could learn how to play, he still needed to learn how to skate.

CHAPTER 9

At 6:03 a.m. the next morning, Jay's alarm woke him up, and he threw off his covers. He was even more excited than he was the day before. He saw each new day, as a day to become a better skater. Jay got dressed as quick as he could, went downstairs, and slid into the kitchen to have his breakfast.

"Morning, little buddy. I don't think we'll be able to go skating today," his grandpa said, as Jay entered the kitchen.

"Why not?" Jay asked.

"Take a look for yourself," Jay's grandpa said gesturing to the window.

Jay leaned far forward up against the counter, so he could see past the glare from the kitchen light. Out the window, he saw millions of big, white snowflakes falling from the sky. Jay had a flash of disappointment, but another idea popped into his head.

"I could skate and shovel the rink, grandpa," Jay said. "I don't even have a stick to skate with, anyway. I'll use the shovel."

Jay's grandpa admired his grandson's determination.

"That could work," his grandpa said heading to the stove. "Let's get you a bowl of brown sugar."

"Sounds good," Jay said and laughed. "Hey, grandpa, will grandma and my mom be coming down again?"

"Don't count on it, little buddy," his grandpa said as he prepared Jay's breakfast. "That was probably a one-time thing. I'm usually the only one up at this time."

Jay was a bit disappointed that his grandma didn't wake up to score the "game winning goal" again in the kitchen, but he was happy to spend the morning with his grandpa.

After breakfast, Jay and his grandpa got dressed in their winter gear, headed out the back door, and made their way through the gate to the park. As they walked, Jay could feel the large fluffy snowflakes melt on his face. He took deep breaths, and the crisp fresh air filled his lungs. Being outside that early in the morning made him feel awake and alive.

Jay and his grandpa both realized that there was a lot more snow than they thought. The path to the rink was completely covered in snow.

"Step where I step," his grandpa said.

Jay did his best trying to follow in his grandpa's big footsteps all the way to the rink.

Once they got to the rink, Jay laced up his skates, grabbed a yellow shovel that was leaning up against the boards, and stepped on to the ice. Jay couldn't go anywhere without making a path. He had to lean heavily on the shovel, and dig his skates in so that he could push the snow a few feet.

"Pile up the snow along the boards, and I'll scoop it up," his grandpa said, as he stepped on the ice with a big, blue shovel.

Jay started off slow, but he was able to make more progress once he made a big enough path to get some momentum.

Jay and his grandpa spent the next hour clearing off the rink.

When it was time to go, Jay took his skates off, put his boots back on, looked back at the rink, and smiled. "Hey, grandpa, look, all that work for nothing," Jay said. The ice was already covered with snow. But it wasn't for nothing. Shoveling all that snow made him a much stronger skater.

Jay followed in his grandpa's footsteps back across the field, so that he could get home and get ready for school. After what happened the day before, he was not excited to go to school at all. He no longer had a stick to bring with him, and he wasn't ready to see Brendan, or his mean teacher. Unfortunately, he still had to go.

Jay struggled to get to school through the field. His grandpa's big footsteps had already been snowed over, and Jay fell over twice by the time he was halfway there. When he fell, he picked himself up, brushed off the snow, and continued on his way. Once he made it to the rink, he looked over the boards. All the traces that he had been there just over an hour before, had disappeared. That didn't bother him at all. He knew that his morning skate would probably be the best part of his day.

After watching the snow continue to fall on the rink for a few minutes, Jay made the rest of the walk to the school.

As he entered the classroom, Miss Wallace saw him, squinted her eyes, and looked back at her computer screen. Jay could tell that she simply did not like him, and he didn't know why. He had never experienced this at his old school, and it made him feel awful. It made him feel like he would never belong in that classroom. He sat down at his desk, and wished the day was over.

When morning recess arrived, he wasn't able to play hockey, but no one else was able to either. The snow kept falling all morning, and there wasn't a cleared off area for them to play. Jay went back to keeping to himself, and he found his way to the rink. Without having anything else to do, or anyone else to hang out with, he grabbed the yellow shovel that was leaning up against the boards, and continued the job he began earlier that morning.

Jay collected a pile of snow, and started to launch a shovel-full over the boards. "Hey, loser," he heard someone yell. Jay stopped and turned around. He saw Brendan and a few of the other boys at the other end of the rink. "You suck at hockey, and you suck at shoveling, too," Brendan added once he got Jay's attention. The other boys laughed.

What is his problem? Jay wondered. Brendan kept yelling other things, but Jay paid no attention to him, and kept on pushing the snow. Since he didn't react, Brendan and his friends went away.

Jay was relieved when they left, and he was glad he had

something to pass the time. When he was alone every day, the fifteen minutes at recess felt like hours. Jay didn't know if he would ever be able to make friends at school, but he still thought that if he could learn to play hockey, he would have a chance.

In the classroom after recess, Jay struggled to pay attention to his teacher. He started to notice that everything she did was mean. Her lessons consisted of barking orders, embarrassing students, and getting the class to work in complete silence. She took all the joy out of learning. School was a hard place to be.

Jay made it through the rest of the school day and was glad when the day was over. While he packed up his things to make his walk home, Miss Wallace came to his locker to talk to him.

"So, I heard your mother called the school today, and said that she wasn't going to pay for Brendan's stick, since it wasn't your fault," Miss Wallace said.

"It wasn't," Jay replied, and continued to put on his jacket.

"Well, now we know where you get it from."

"Get what from?" Jay said. He was confused.

"The lying. The bad behaviour," Miss Wallace said with a snarl.

My mom never lies and she is not a bad person, Jay thought.

"Now I have to call Brendan's parents," Miss Wallace continued, "and explain that you are refusing to pay for his stick even though you broke it." She then walked away and muttered, "Why is it always the single moms and their kids that are the problem?"

Jay didn't know exactly what she meant by this, but he knew it wasn't a nice thing to say. He thought about going home and telling his mom, but he also didn't want to hurt her feelings.

He zipped up his jacket, put his tuque and gloves on, went outside, and plowed his way across the field.

Jay was out of breath as he got to his grandparent's backyard. With all the snow that fell, he had to shove the back gate open and shove the gate closed. There was a loud *clank* as the metal latch slammed into place. His grandpa must have heard the noise, and he came out of the garage. He was holding the broken stick from the day before, but now it had a blue plastic blade attached.

"Grandpa, you fixed it!" Jay said. He trudged his way through the snow to where his grandpa was standing.

"Your Uncle Dylan and his friends all had these plastic blades on their old sticks for street hockey," his grandpa said. "This one you can use outside." He handed Jay the stick.

"Thanks, grandpa!" Jay said.

"You're welcome, little buddy. But you should go inside. Your mom has another surprise for you."

"What is it?"

"I can't tell you that! Go in and see for yourself."

Jay ran to the back door, flung it open, and went inside. He was still carrying his hockey stick with the plastic blade.

"Mom, look what grandpa gave me!" he said as he got in the door. He didn't even know where his mom was in the house. He kicked off his boots, and dropped his bag down on top of them. He was too excited to bother putting them away.

His mom came from the living room to greet her son. "Oh, look at that. Your grandpa put on a new blade. That was very nice of him," his mom said.

"Check it out!" Jay said, and held the blade up to show her.

"Looks very nice," she said and smiled. "Did you thank your grandpa?"

"Sure did!"

"Well, I think you're going to like what I got you, too."

"What is it?" Jay asked.

"Go look in your room," Jay's mom said.

Jay raced towards the stairs and ran up as fast as he could, but he also made sure he didn't hit the walls with his stick on the way up. His mom followed carefully behind with a smile on her face. She always loved to see how excited he would get over the littlest things. He was always a very grateful son.

Jay opened his bedroom door and there was a brand-new, yellow, Easton Synergy hockey stick lying flat on his bed. Jay's eyes grew wide in delight. Still holding the old stick in his right hand, he picked up the new one in his left.

"Whoa! It's so light," he said, and he tossed the old stick onto his bed. He held the new stick in both hands and waved it around in front of him.

Jay's mom walked in, but kept a safe distance away. "This is for me?" Jay asked.

"It sure is, kiddo," his mom said. "Your uncle Dylan helped pick it out today. He said that this was the model he had when he was younger, and they haven't made this stick in years...but they brought it back this hockey season, or something. Your uncle was really excited about it."

"This is awesome...thank you, mom!"

He went over to her carrying his new stick, and gave her a hug.

"Careful with that thing," she said as he wrapped his arms and stick around her. "You can use the one with the plastic blade outside, and at school, and your new one you can use on the ice in the morning when you practice...how does that sound?"

"Sounds good to me," Jay said releasing his mom. He started to examine every inch of his new stick. Everything about it impressed Jay—from the crisp, white tape on the knob to the flawlessly wrapped black tape around the blade. He ran his fingers along the blade.

"Your uncle taped that for you," his mom said. "It took him awhile, but he wanted it to be perfect."

Jay thought it was perfect. Everything was perfect. He was so happy, he forgot to tell his mom what his teacher had said to him after school. As far he was concerned, his mom was the best and nicest mom in the entire world.

Now that he had two hockey sticks, Jay wanted to start practicing his shooting. So that night, his grandpa set him up in the garage with his uncle's old hockey net. Jay watched as his grandpa tied old metal hubcaps in the top right and left corners of the net.

"What are those for?" Jay asked.

"Target practice," his grandpa said. "Each time you hit one of those, it will sound like this—" His grandpa took a hammer from his work bench and hit the hubcap. *Clang!*

Jay cringed at the noise. He wasn't used to it yet. But he soon would be.

"That was a lot louder than I thought," his grandpa said with a chuckle.

At first his grandpa was thrilled when he heard the *Clang!* coming from the garage. That meant his grandson was getting better. But not long after, Jay got too good at it. His grandpa worried that the entire neighbourhood would complain about the *Clang! Clang! Clang!* coming from their garage every night.

CHAPTER 10

The next day, Jay brought his wooden hockey stick with the plastic blade to school. Even though the last time playing hockey at recess didn't go well, he still wanted to play hockey and make friends. Jay put his stick behind the door with all the rest, and waited impatiently all morning for that first bell.

When the bell rang, it was like a starting pistol. The boys bolted from their desks, put on their winter gear in a flash, grabbed their sticks, and charged outside. In the rush, Jay was right there with them, and he threw his stick into the pile with the rest.

Unfortunately, Brendan saw the plastic blade immediately. "Hey, look, Jay's crappy stick is even crappier. But that makes sense since his mom is poor," Brendan said, and held out the stick like a trophy.

"My mom's not poor," Jay said.

"That's what my mom told me," Brendan said. "She said your mom is a poor single mom and couldn't afford to buy me a new stick...even though you owe me one. And she clearly couldn't buy you a new stick after I broke your crappy stick."

This was the second time that someone mentioned that his mom was a poor single mom. *Why did they keep saying that?* Jay wondered.

"I knew you broke mine," Jay said. "And it wasn't even mine, it was my uncle's. Just wait until I tell him what you did."

"Oh, I'm so scared. What is some old guy going to come beat me up?" Brendan stepped toward Jay. "How about I beat the crap out of you right now."

Jay remembered what his uncle Dylan showed him the other night, but he wasn't ready to get into his first fight. As Brendan headed towards him, Jay took a couple steps back.

"Can we just play already," another boy said. "We barely have enough time as it is."

"We'll continue this another time, loser," Brendan said. Suddenly, he put his left arm way out in front of his face, pulled his right hand way back, and threw Jay's stick like a javelin as far as he could into a snow bank.

Jay ran over to get it, and he hurried back to put it in the pile with all the other sticks. Jay was relieved that he didn't get into a fight with Brendan. But he was worried about when Brendan would try again.

Once all the sticks were in the pile, a boy with a bright orange tuque over his face tossed out the sticks, and the teams were picked. This recess, Jay and Brendan were on the same team.

"You better not suck, loser," Brendan said as they picked up their sticks. Brendan was upset that they were on the same team. But Jay was glad because he knew that Brendan couldn't do anything to his own teammate. At least he hoped he couldn't.

The game finally started, and Jay had a lot of fun playing. He was a great defenseman like he was two days before. At one point, he even passed the ball to Brendan, and Brendan ran really fast past their defence, scored a goal, tripped and fell, but popped up and celebrated. It was a great goal, and Jay and Brendan's team won that recess 5-3.

Jay thought that maybe everything would be better if him and Brendan were on the same team. Maybe they could get along.

But during class shortly before lunch, Jay's hopes faded away. Miss Wallace was walking up and down the rows like a shark looking for its next meal. As she passed Brendan's desk, she noticed there was blood on Brendan's jeans. "What happened, Brendan?" she asked.

Brendan looked down and saw the blood. "Oh, that. Jay tripped me at recess."

"Why didn't you tell me he did this?" Miss Wallace asked.

"I forgot," Brendan said shrugging his shoulders.

Jay couldn't believe what he was hearing. He didn't trip Brendan—they were on the same team. Brendan fell after scoring a great goal, and Jay was the one that passed him the ball and got the assist.

"Jay Noble, go out to the hallway. Right now!" Miss Wallace shouted.

Jay jumped in his desk. Her scream startled him.

Jay got out of his desk, and slowly walked out of the classroom. He could feel all the eyes of his classmates on him.

Miss Wallace shut the door.

"Why can't you play well with the other boys? You broke Brendan's stick the other day, and you and your mom lied about it. And now you tripped him and made him bleed?" Miss Wallace said with her scrunched-up face and crooked teeth.

Jay was surprised how fast his teacher's face turned red when she was angry. "I didn't trip him. We were on the same team," Jay said.

"Now why would he lie about something like this?"

"I don't know. You would have to ask him."

Miss Wallace stood there starring. It was making Jay uncomfortable. It felt like she was trying to shoot laser beams out of her eyes.

"Once again, now we have to go call your mom," she said.

"Please don't." He felt a lump in his throat.

"So, you did do it?" Miss Wallace asked. She looked satisfied that she got him to confess.

"No. But my mom has school today, and I don't want her to worry about another one of Brendan's lies."

Miss Wallace's face started to turn red again. "This is just too big of a deal not to call home. You hurt another student on purpose. But I'll let the principal deal with you. Off we go."

Jay put his head down and started to walk down the hallway. There was no winning with this teacher. She automatically took Brendan's side every time. She was just as bad as the class bully. Maybe even worse.

All Jay wanted to do was have fun playing hockey with his classmates at recess, but Brendan would always find a way to ruin it. It didn't matter if they were on the same team. It didn't matter if what Brendan said was a lie. Jay was the one in trouble.

Miss Wallace brought Jay to the principal once again, and the principal called his mom. He had to serve another in-school suspension in the principal's office.

After getting in trouble at school the second time, there weren't any new gifts from his grandpa or mom, instead they were frustrated. Jay didn't know if they were frustrated at him, Brendan, or the school. They said they believed him when he told his side of what happened, but eventually that changed.

For three full weeks, Jay kept on playing hockey at recess. But the other boys in his class started to blame everything on Jay, and his teacher always took their side. It was no longer about playing hockey at recess for the other kids—instead it became a competition on who could get Jay in the most trouble. Day after day, someone would come in from recess and say things like: *Jay tripped me; Jay swore at me; Jay slashed me with his stick; Jay punched me.*

Jay's mom received phone call after phone call.

CHAPTER 11

Jay spent many nights shooting pucks in the garage. He would take 33 wrist shots, 33 backhands, and 33 slapshots. He counted every shot, and it was always in that same order. If he wanted to keep on shooting, he would start over with 33 wrist shots, and would always have to end off back on 99—it was like a game that helped him get better. Counting each shot also helped him forget any of the issues he was having at school.

Jay was also starting to learn a lot more about hockey. He spent his free time reading books about Gordie Howe and Wayne Gretzky, and watching Toronto Maple Leafs games with his grandpa and Uncle Dylan. Hockey was becoming a big part of his life.

One night when Jay came in the house from hitting the hubcaps 99 times, he heard his mom, grandma, and grandpa talking about him in the living room.

"I don't know what to do with him," Jay heard his mom say. "I know that moving has been tough, but I didn't raise him to pick on other kids and lie all the time. He was never like this in Calgary. Maybe we should have never moved back to Saskatoon. Maybe we should move back there and I could go back to working. At least Jay was much happier there."

Jay stood at the back entrance and felt awful. All this time he had been doing nothing wrong, but his mom didn't believe him anymore. Jay thought that his grandparents would at least come to his defense, but they didn't.

"None of our kids were like this. Your brother got in a bit of trouble later in high school, but he was never like Jay," his grandma said.

"What I don't understand is that he is so sweet at home. It's like he is a completely different kid from how he is at school," his mom said.

"That's almost the scariest part. How can he be two different people like that?" his grandma added.

"Maybe we have to move him to another school. Maybe things will be better there," he heard his grandpa say.

Jay felt like everything was falling apart. He had no one on his side. No friends, no teachers, and not even his family. Maybe a new school would be better. But it should be the other boys that had to move schools. Why could they get away with everything?

His family was silent for a while. Jay didn't know if he should slip back outside quietly, or if he should try and make a loud entrance. He decided to open and close the door loudly, and stomp his boots. He wanted to make sure his family heard him this time.

Jay walked past the living room without looking at them. He couldn't stand to face them after what he just heard them saying. He knew if he went to talk to them, he would probably start to cry.

"Jay, you're not even going to come say hi to us?" he heard his mom say from the living room.

"Sorry…can't…homework," Jay said as he ran up the stairs to his room.

He flopped onto his bed, rolled over, and stared at the ceiling. He felt lost. He felt alone. He felt like his family didn't want him.

Eventually, he got up, and looked out the window. He watched all the other kids skating on the rink. He wished he could be out there with them, but he wasn't ready yet.

Later that night, Jay knocked on his mom's bedroom door, and opened it a little. His mom was sitting up in her bed reading. "Mom, can I talk to you?"

"Of course," she said. Jay seemed to still be her polite little boy. She remembered what her own mom said earlier: *That's almost the scariest part. How can he be like two different people like that?*

He came and sat on the edge of her bed. "I heard you and grandma and grandpa talking earlier, and I've been thinking. Can I go live with my dad?"

Hearing her son say that came as a shock. "Oh, Jay-Jay, I'm sorry you had to hear that," she said, and put her book down beside her. "Your grandma, grandpa, and I don't know what to do. This has all been so stressful on us. And no, you can't go live your dad. Your dad has his own family in Calgary. But you're my baby, and the thought of you going anywhere else would make me very sad. I love you, and we will figure all this out together, okay?"

It was a relief hearing her say that. He didn't actually want to go live with his dad, but he thought his mom didn't want him anymore. "Okay," he said and moved up on the bed and snuggled up to her. "Mom, can I ask you something?"

"Anything, my Jay-Jay," she said.

"I know you're not with my dad, but why don't you find someone else? You're still young and pretty."

Jay's mom didn't know how to answer that question to an eleven-year-old. Her boy was the caring and kind kid that he had always been. *At least he didn't lose that yet,* she thought.

"Awe, Jay, you are so sweet. Maybe some day. Right now, I want to focus on going to school, and getting a good job so I can take care of us. Buy a big house, and buy you all the two-hundred and fifty dollar hockey sticks that you want."

"But I like living with grandma and grandpa," Jay said. He slid out of his mom's bed and stood up. "It would be nice to have all those sticks though."

His mom smiled. Jay was able to cheer his mom up, and his mom was able to cheer him up. They still needed each other—no matter what was going on at school.

CHAPTER 12

The next morning, Jay felt lonelier than ever. Even though his mom made him feel better, he still knew that he was causing his family stress. Yet, he didn't know how to stop it. He no longer felt like he had a place where he belonged. He hated going to school, and he felt bad about being at home. The only place where he felt truly happy was for one hour in the mornings when he was skating on the rink. But all of that would end the moment he got to school.

Jay dreaded making that walk past the hockey rink, to his school, and into class. He knew that he wasn't going to go live with his dad, but like his grandpa suggested, maybe he should at least move schools. Any school, and any teacher had to be better than the one he had. Jay made up his mind that he would talk to his mom that evening about switching schools as soon as possible.

Those were the thoughts Jay had as he went to school that day, and they continued as he sat in his desk. He found himself looking around the classroom, at the other students, at his teacher, and thinking, *there isn't anything here for me.* When the bell rang for the first recess, Jay stood up from his desk.

"Jay, I need to talk to you for a second," Miss Wallace said as the class was leaving for recess.

"Shocking. Jay is in trouble again," Brendan said, and him and his friends laughed as they grabbed their jackets, hockey sticks, and left the room.

Jay's face turned red. *What now?* he thought.

"Jay, I want to talk to you about hockey," Miss Wallace said as everyone left the classroom. "I know some of the other boys have been picking on you…so I want to have a little chat. Listen, Jay, these boys have been playing hockey since they were in kindergarten, and they are very good. I understand you like hockey, and want to play, but you just don't fit in with them. You will only get in their way, and you will keep getting hurt. You get it, don't you?"

"So…so I can't play with them?" Jay asked. He was trying to understand what she was saying to him.

"I don't think it's a good idea," Miss Wallace said.

"What am I supposed to do at recess? All the boys play hockey."

"You can find something else to do by yourself. Now run along. I have to go talk to the principal about another matter," she said, and pointed to the door.

Jay felt like there was a giant lump in his throat. He felt like he was going to cry. He hoped he could hold it in until he made it to the bathroom. Jay put his jacket hood over his head and looked at the ground as he walked hurriedly down the hallway. Tears were already falling down his face.

"Jay, watch out!" Ava, a young girl in his class, shrieked.

Ava Berwin was pretty, popular, and smart. She had long brown hair, big brown eyes, and a kind smile. All the other boys in his class tried to get her attention—when they weren't playing hockey, that is. She was nice and always said "hi" to Jay ever since his first day at the school. But her friends weren't that nice. They were loud and would pick on some of the other girls. Jay did notice that Ava never joined in when her friends were being mean, and she never laughed at him when everyone else did.

Jay stopped, and looked up just before he ran into Ava in the hallway. She saw the tears, and he was embarrassed.

"Are you okay?" Ava asked gently with her kind smile.

For some reason he wanted to tell her that he wasn't. He wanted to tell her what happened. He wanted to tell her how he was feeling. But he barely even knew her. He thought she was probably just like all the other kids in his class.

"Leave me alone," Jay said. He put his head down, and walked past her.

Jay felt bad about being mean to Ava. He made it to the bathroom, but he was feeling even worse than before.

He was glad to see that no one else was in the bathroom. This bathroom was surprisingly clean. It had a tiled floor that sparkled, and the bathroom stalls were freshly painted blue. Even the garbage can was empty. This was the opposite of the bathrooms at Jay's old school in Calgary—this one looked like it was hardly used. This bathroom was nice. Maybe a little too nice.

Jay went into the third stall at the very end, and locked the door. That stall would become his stall. Unfortunately, since he wasn't able to play hockey at recess, he would go on to spend more time in there than any young boy should.

CHAPTER 13

For the next week, Jay spent nearly every recess in that bathroom stall feeling sad and lonely. Eventually the sadness went away, and Jay started to read books about hockey in his little hideout. That became his escape. While he read, he could pretend that he was one of the many great hockey players that he read about.

No one seemed to notice that he didn't go outside for recess—not the other boys in his class, and definitely not his teacher.

But one day, Ava walked past his desk, smiled at him, and placed a folded piece of paper on his worksheet. Jay snatched up the piece of paper, and carefully unfolded it in his desk. He slid down a little in his seat, so that he could read the note.

Hi, Jay, I noticed you don't go outside for recess!! Are you hiding???
From: Ava.

Jay read the note over three times. The writing on the note was in perfect, purple ink, and there was a little heart after Ava's name. Jay had butterflies in his stomach, and he was actually surprised that someone noticed that he wasn't going out for recess. But he knew that she was one of the popular students, and her friends were often mean to him. Then he came to the realization that it must have been some sort of joke. The butterflies in his stomach flew away.

He flipped the note over, and wrote his reply as neat as possible: *None of your business.* He folded the note carefully.

Ava sat in the row next to his, but she was three desks back. Jay didn't know how he was going to get the note to her. He thought about making a detour to the pencil sharpener. Then he imagined that if this was all a big joke, they were probably planning to trip him or something. He decided to play it safe. He decided it was best to forget about her and her note. He slipped the note into his pocket, and tried to forget about it.

When the bell rang to mark the end of the day, Jay packed up as quick as possible, and headed out the door.

"Jay, wait up!" he heard someone say as he was about to walk across the field.

He turned around, and it was Ava. Surprisingly, the butterflies came back. "Why didn't you reply to my note?" Ava said when she caught up to him.

Jay remembered the note in his pocket.

"I did reply," he said, and reached in his pocket and handed her the note. He turned and kept on walking. Jay didn't trust her. Jay didn't really trust anybody anymore.

Ava unfolded and read the note, and then ran to catch up with him again. "I know it's none of my business," she said. "And I'm sorry...I didn't mean to upset you."

Jay stopped and looked at her. She was wearing a light purple tuque, and her bright brown eyes lit up her face. He didn't know why she wouldn't leave him alone. But he could tell by her gentle smile, that she wasn't trying to play a joke on him or hurt him.

"I'm sorry I was being rude to you," Jay said. "But I don't know what you want."

"I wanted to talk to you. We are practically neighbours, you know?" Ava said, and smiled again. "I've watched you from my bedroom window on the rink in the morning."

"You have?" Jay's face turned red. He never imagined that someone would see his morning practices.

They both started walking across the field.

"You're getting much better," Ava said.

"You've seen me out there more than once?"

"Just a few dozen times or so."

Jay laughed. "What are you doing up so early?"

"My dad wakes up really early to go to work, and I always hear him. Sometimes I can go back to sleep, other times I can't. And those times I can't, I watch you. I sound like a creep, don't I?"

"Maybe a little," Jay said teasingly. "My grandpa wakes up really early too. But I don't know why. I think it's cause he is old or something."

"He's the one out there with you in the morning?"

"That's him."

"Why do you practice so early?" Ava asked.

"I, uh—" Jay stammered. He didn't know what to say, but decided to tell her the truth. "I practice so early because I'm learning how to skate. After school it's always so busy, and I don't want anyone to see me."

"You did look a little rusty the first time I saw you out there," she said.

"How bad was I?"

"Let's just say I saw you fall a lot. I may have actually giggled a few times."

Jay felt a little embarrassed but he knew she wasn't trying to be mean. "That's why I didn't want to try to learn how to skate in front of anyone. Could you imagine if someone like Brendan saw me?"

"Forget about him. Brendan is a jerk," Ava said.

"I thought you were sort of friends with him?" Jay asked.

"No!" Ava replied in disgust. "He tries to be my friend, but the only reason why is because his parents are friends with my parents. So, whenever they come over, he always comes over. Or when my parents go there, they bring me. I can't stand him!"

Jay was relieved to hear that.

Ava continued. "And what he is doing to you is so awful. Someone needs to do something about it. I tried to tell my parents, and all they said was, 'Brendan would never do that.' I don't know what it is about him, but it's like he can get away with anything."

"Exactly! And Miss Wallace never believes me when I tell her what actually happened."

"She's awful, too! Everyone knows she is the meanest teacher in the school," Ava said.

"My family used to believe me, but now they are starting to think that I am doing all these terrible things at school, and then lying about it. I heard them talking about me the other day. I think I am going to move schools," Jay said.

"No! I don't want you to move schools."

"Why not?" Jay asked.

"Because I would miss you," Ava said.

Jay didn't know what to say. He still didn't know why she was being so nice to him.

"Why would you miss me? You barely know me."

"Because you are the nicest boy in our class, and I'm tired of being around such mean people all the time."

"Your friends are kind of mean, too. Aren't they?" Jay said.

"Yes, they are, and I don't know why," Ava replied. "You know what?"

"What?" Jay said.

"I think we should be friends. We can be nice together," Ava said excitedly.

"I would like that."

"It's set then. We are friends. And thanks for walking me home," Ava said.

Without Jay paying attention while they talked, he all of sudden realized that he was standing outside of Ava's back yard.

"I'll see you tomorrow," Ava said with a smile.

"See you tomorrow," Jay said and smiled back.

Jay walked the distance of four backyards to his grandparent's gate. The whole time he felt happier than he did in a while. He had been at the school for half the year, and never made one friend. Out of nowhere, Ava became his friend. He decided he would try to stay at that school for her.

But the next day, Brendan and the boys almost took things too far.

CHAPTER 14

Jay stepped on the ice and his skates carved up the freshly flooded rink. It was a beautiful morning—and to Jay—a perfect morning. He didn't have to shovel, which meant he could spend the entire time out there working on his skills. The day before, his grandpa showed him how to do crossovers, and Jay blazed around the rink cutting and circling around. Jay was a hard worker, but for some reason, he pushed himself even harder that morning. Maybe it was because Ava could be watching.

Jay's grandpa started to notice that Jay was becoming a pretty special skater. He was getting faster and smoother every day. His grandpa tossed out a puck, and Jay took it and practiced his stick handling as he circled around. Jay sped around the rink handling the puck with his head up, and did things that normally took years of practice. Jay had only been skating for almost two months. His grandpa couldn't believe it. *This kid can really play hockey*, his grandpa thought that morning. Jay was a natural.

"I think we will have to sign you up for hockey next year, little buddy," Jay's grandpa said when Jay sat down to untie his skates.

"That would be so awesome," Jay said.

"You're ready. More than ready. You were pretty amazing out there today."

"Thanks, grandpa," Jay said as he pulled on his boots.

Jay also felt like he was getting better—he rarely fell, and he was having a lot more fun out there. He hoped Ava was watching that morning.

When Jay left for school, he decided to wait by his back gate so he could walk with Ava. He was excited to have a friend, and he wanted to see if she watched him skate that morning.

He was kicking the snow—for what felt like forever—when he finally saw Ava appear from her backyard. Jay ran over to catch up with her.

"Good morning, Ava," Jay greeted her as he got closer.

"Good morning," Ava said. "I'm glad you're the one running after me today, since you made me run after you yesterday," she said, and pushed his arm.

"I don't mind running," Jay said and smiled.

"I'm surprised you could still run after the practice you had this morning."

"I was wondering if you were watching."

"I was. You looked great out there."

Hearing Ava compliment him made his morning. He felt taller.

"How about we meet at eight thirty each morning and we can walk together?" Jay asked.

"That sounds great," Ava replied, and they continued walking. "So, are you ever going to tell me where you've been hiding at recess?"

Jay didn't know if he should tell her or not. He felt embarrassed, but he also found it easy to talk to Ava. "I've been hanging out in the bathroom. Miss Wallace said I wasn't allowed to play hockey at recess, and she told me to find something to do on my own. So, I've been sitting in there and reading books."

"That's awful! Is that why you were crying in the hallway that one day?"

"I wasn't crying! I had something in my eye," Jay said.

"Oh, yes. I hate it when that happens," Ava said smiling. "Anyway, you don't have to hide in the bathroom anymore. We can hang out at recess."

"What about your friends?" Jay asked.

"Forget about them. I would rather spend time with you," Ava said.

"I would rather spend time with you, too."

"Oh, that's sweet. I feel so special. You would rather spend time with me than in a bathroom," Ava said sarcastically.

"You know what I mean!" Jay said, and held the school door open for Ava.

"I do. I'm just teasing you," Ava said and stomped her feet as she entered the school.

Jay and Ava walked into the class together and sat down at their desks. Jay had a smile on his face for the first time at school since he brought that wooden stick for recess hockey.

During class in the morning, Miss Wallace had to leave the room. She left the room more than any other teacher that Jay had back in Calgary. While she was gone, Brendan, Ryan, and Tyson got out of their desks, grabbed their sticks from behind the door, and started to play hockey at the front of the class with a crumpled-up piece of paper. They were fooling around to a number of laughs when Brendan and Tyson bumped into the teacher's desk, and the computer monitor fell and smashed on the ground. Brendan tried to pick it up, but Ryan warned him that the teacher was coming. Tyson and Ryan rushed to put their sticks behind the door and ran to their desks.

When Miss Wallace walked in, Brendan was still holding the computer monitor and his hockey stick was on the floor beside him. "What is going on here?" she hollered and charged in with heavy footsteps.

She was angry a lot, but the class had never seen her this angry before. *Finally*, Jay thought. *Finally, someone else was going to get in trouble for once.*

"It was Jay!" Brendan yelled in a panic. "He knocked over your computer then ran to his desk. I'm just trying to pick it up for you." He put the monitor back on the ground and walked back to his desk as if he did nothing wrong. He left his hockey stick right there on the floor.

Miss Wallace didn't attempt to ask anyone else what happened. No one else said that Brendan was lying. His teacher turned to look at Jay, and said in a very deep and angry voice, "Get over here."

The teacher looked so terrifying that everyone froze. And it was so quiet, you could hear a pin drop. Jay wanted to stay in his desk, but he stood up and walked over sheepishly. He was scared. Very scared. As he reached the teacher's desk, Miss Wallace looked at him with gritted teeth. "Now look what you did," she said. Everyone watched in complete silence—they were afraid to make any kind of sound. "Look how damaged the computer screen is," she added as she bent over to pick it up.

That's when the most shocking thing happened. As Miss Wallace bent down to pick up the broken computer monitor, she let out a loud rumbling fart that squeaked like a mouse at the end. Jay, the teacher, and everyone else couldn't believe what just happened.

"Gross," Jay said. He was standing right in the line of fire, and the smell of rotten eggs filled his nose.

"Nasty," another girl shrieked.

"Disgusting," someone else groaned.

But the rest of the room, mostly the boys, roared with laughter.

Miss Wallace straightened-up and had a beet-red face. "Jay Noble, I can't believe you just did that!" she screamed. "You are a disturbed young boy. Get to the principal's office. Now!" she commanded while pointing at the door.

"That wasn't me, that was you," Jay replied. He couldn't believe she was trying to blame him. *If that came out of me, I would have exploded*, he thought. Jay didn't know what to do, but he couldn't stand staying in that area any longer. He covered his nose and walked back to his desk.

"You're gross," one of Ava's friends said.

"Nice one, Noble," one of the boys called out with a grin.

Jay was embarrassed. They all thought it was him. He was too afraid to look at Ava. He felt like running away, and never coming back.

Jay sat down at his desk and looked straight ahead.

"Get to the principal's office," Miss Wallace yelled at Jay with even more anger than before.

Jay looked up at his teacher. "No," Jay said. "I didn't do anything."

The class fell completely silent again. They all waited to see what would happen next.

Miss Wallace walked toward Jay and stood over him. "Get up right now."

Jay saw that her fists were clenched. And if this was a cartoon, there would have been steam coming out of her ears. "No," he said again.

With lightning speed, his teacher grabbed him by the sweater, and yanked him out of his desk. Jay was stunned. Without any more resistance, Miss Wallace marched him out of class.

Jay walked down the hallway feeling like her prisoner. Things kept on getting worse, and it didn't matter that he finally made a friend. He needed to move schools.

CHAPTER 15

There was another trip to the principal's office, and Jay's mom got another call. This time Jay was sent home and suspended for two days. They also said that his mom would have to pay to replace the computer monitor.

When Jay got home, his mom met him at the door, and she was angrier than he had ever seen her. "No more practices, no more hockey, you can go sit in your room," she yelled. She didn't even give him a chance to explain himself.

Jay ran upstairs to his room and slammed the door. Everyone seemed to be against him again.

Eventually Jay tried to pass the time by doing some homework and reading a hockey book, but he kept thinking about what happened that day. He was upset with Brendan and his teacher. He couldn't believe how horrible they were.

Around lunchtime, while Jay was still in his room, the doorbell rang, but Jay paid no attention to it. About ten minutes later, his mom knocked gently on his door, and opened it. "Jay, can you come downstairs with me for a minute," she said.

Jay followed his mom down the stairs, and his mom led the way to the living room. She didn't look angry anymore.

When they got there, he was surprised to see Ava sitting on his grandparent's couch. She was still wearing her light purple tuque and her new purple jacket.

"Jay, look who is here," his mom said.

"Hi, Jay," Ava said.

"Hi, Ava, what are you doing here?" Jay asked. He wasn't

asking in a mean way, he truly wanted to know what she was doing there.

"Well, Jay," his mom said. "Ava just finished telling me something interesting. She said that what happened today was not your fault. She said you were sitting at your desk when three boys broke your teacher's computer. She also said that these same boys have been lying and blaming you for things you didn't do this entire school year. She also said that the teacher tried blaming you, for, well, something very unpleasant she did today, too." Jay's mom tried not to laugh as she said the last part, and then carried on. "Ava knew it wasn't fair, and ran here at lunchtime to come tell me herself."

Jay instantly felt like the entire world was lifted off his shoulders. "I told you, mom."

"I'm so sorry I didn't believe you, Jay-Jay," his mom said. "Ava even tells me that your teacher picks on you and is mean to you quite often. I'm so sorry this is happening to you."

Jay felt a number of different emotions. He was relieved that his mom knew the truth, and she actually believed him. He was also upset that she didn't believe him this whole time, and that he had to suffer on his own for so long.

"I better get home and eat lunch," Ava said as she stood up. "I hope to see you at school soon, Jay."

"Thank you so much, Ava," he said. He watched her as she put on her purple and white boots. She gave him a little wave and a smile and went out the front door. Jay was so grateful for what Ava did. He had a feeling that things would get better.

Jay, his mom, grandma, and grandpa discussed all the different options about what to do next as they ate lunch.

When his grandpa heard that these boys were the ones actually blaming Jay for all these things he didn't do, he was furious. He was even more furious when he found out that Jay's teacher was just as bad, and he almost hit the roof when he heard she yanked Jay out of his desk by his sweater. They all agreed that something needed to be done about this teacher, but it wasn't as easy as simply saying it. By the end of lunch, it was decided that Jay's mom would call the principal, and arrange to have a meeting with her the next day in person. Until then, Jay was still suspended.

CHAPTER 16

Since Ava explained everything that was happening to Jay, he was no longer in trouble. Even though he was still suspended from school, he was able to go for his morning practice, and shoot pucks in the garage. To Jay, that was much better than going to school.

When Jay's mom got home from a meeting with the principal that afternoon, Jay and his grandma and grandpa were all eager to hear the news. Jay was sitting at the table drinking hot chocolate with his grandma when his mom came home.

His mom walked into the kitchen, grabbed a glass from the cupboard, and filled it with water at the sink. Then his grandpa walked in from the living room with a cup of coffee.

"So, what did she say, mom?" Jay asked.

"Well," his mom said walking over to the table with her glass of water. She took a sip, and then put the glass down. "Your principal pretty much said that she would look into these accusations."

"Accusations!" Jay's grandpa said raising his voice. "They are more than accusations. Those boys and the teacher have been bullying Jay all year."

"That's what I told her, dad," his mom said. "When I brought up how Jay's teacher yanked him out of his desk, she said this was a serious accusation, and could have an impact on her career. I told the principal that I understood that. But if she has been doing the things she is doing, she could have a serious impact on her students' lives. The principal didn't know how to respond to that.

To be honest, I got the feeling she simply didn't want to go ahead with all the extra work looking into these things. She told me she was retiring at the end of the year."

"What a way to retire," his grandma said. "Knowing you did nothing when a kid was getting bullied?"

"Exactly," Jay's mom said. "She should have retired before she decided it was too much to do her job."

"So, what happens now?" Jay asked. "Do I go back to school?

"Your principal said you are welcome to come back tomorrow," his mom said.

"But, mom, I don't want to go back there."

"We don't really have a choice, Jay," his mom said.

"Can't I go to a different school?" Jay asked.

"I can look into that. But you will have to go back to your school in the meantime," his mom replied.

Jay didn't want to go back and see his teacher again. But at least he would be able to see Ava. Jay's mom, grandma, and grandpa kept on talking about his mom's conversation with the principal, but Jay wasn't interested. He went back out to the garage to shoot 99 pucks.

The next day, Jay walked over and met Ava at her backyard, so they could walk to school together.

"Good morning, stranger," Ava said when she opened the back gate and saw him waiting for her. "How was your two-day vacation?"

"Good morning! Pretty good actually. My new best friend told my mom what has been going on at school. And yesterday, my mom had a meeting with the principal about our teacher."

"Sounds like a pretty great best friend!"

"She is great," Jay stopped walking and looked at Ava. "Seriously, though. Thanks again for doing that, Ava."

"Anytime best friend," Ava said. "Could you imagine if we

got a new teacher?"

"That would be amazing," Jay said, and they kept on making their way to school. Jay had hope that things would get better, and it was all because of Ava.

When school started, Miss Wallace started the day very differently than usual. The principal must have spoken to her after the meeting with Jay's mom. Miss Wallace tried to get the whole class to turn against Jay.

"Good morning, class," she said walking to the front of the room. "It looks like Jay is back today. And now that he is back, I wanted to discuss what happened the other day."

Of course she is going to try and apologize, Jay thought. But that wasn't the case at all.

Miss Wallace continued. "Do you all remember when Jay was out of control and broke my computer screen, and I had to pull him out of his desk because I had to protect you all? Well, that was an unfortunate situation caused by Jay. Because of this, Mrs. Clarke may ask some of you what happened the other day. If she does, please make sure you tell her that I did what I had to do, to keep all of you safe from Jay."

What is she talking about? Jay wondered. *We all need to be kept safe from her!* Jay sat in his desk in disbelief.

"But Jay didn't break your monitor," Ava blurted out. Everybody in the class turned to look at her. "It was Brendan, Ryan, and Tyson that were fooling around with their hockey sticks, and they knocked over your monitor. And you yanked Jay out of his desk for no reason."

Miss Wallace's face twisted with anger. "Ava Berwin, don't think I haven't noticed that you have been talking and walking with Jay. Do you have a crush on him? Is that why you are telling this lie right now?"

"I am not lying," Ava said. "Jay did absolutely nothing. He hasn't done anything at all to get in trouble this whole year. It has always been Brendan, Ryan, Tyson, and some of the others. You simply don't care enough to notice."

"Ava, are you wanting to go to the principal's office?" Miss Wallace threatened.

"For what, telling the truth?" Ava said.

"She is telling the truth," a quiet girl named, Michelle, said.

Others followed and spoke up against their teacher.

Miss Wallace looked around the room. "What is this? What kind of game are you playing here?"

"There isn't a game. I didn't do anything," Jay said. "You're the one trying to get a whole class to lie for you because you're scared you might get fired."

The class went silent, and Miss Wallace went from bright red, to white as a ghost. She hurriedly walked over to her desk, grabbed her purse, and left the classroom. As soon as she left, everyone cheered.

Miss Wallace's plan backfired, and for the first time, it felt like the class was on Jay's side.

Mrs. Clarke came into the classroom shortly after, and said that Miss Wallace went home ill for the day. Mrs. Clarke went on to tell the class that she would be covering for their teacher.

Even though Mrs. Clarke suspended Jay two days before, he was relieved that he didn't have to worry about Miss Wallace—at least for the day. He also didn't have to worry too much about Brendan picking on him in front of the principal.

If it wasn't for Ava standing up for him again, who knows what would have happened.

Jay finally felt like he had people in his corner. And the next morning, he found out someone else was on his side.

CHAPTER 17

The next morning there was a small skiff of snow on the rink. Jay cruised around the ice with the yellow shovel, and cleared the way for his morning skate. It only took him a few minutes, and then he started practicing. While he performed his drills—some he made up and some his grandpa taught him—he looked like he had been skating for years. Nobody would ever be able to tell that he had only learned to skate a few months before.

Jay finished doing a few minutes of quick stops and starts, and he leaned up against the boards to catch his breath. With the earlier sunrises, Jay and his grandpa were often greeted with beautiful Saskatchewan skies. He gazed at the sky and noticed the sun made the clouds look like pink and orange cotton candy.

After the events of the day before, Jay felt like there was a bright future for him in Saskatoon. Now that his mom, grandma, and grandpa knew the truth, he didn't have to feel ashamed. Now that he had a friend at school, his time at school didn't have to be as bad. He pushed off the boards, and kept skating.

When it was time, his grandpa called him in, and Jay finished up his practice. He was out there a little longer than usual, but like most mornings, he was dripping in sweat. He still had to get home, get cleaned up, get ready for school, and then meet Ava at her backyard gate. Walking with her to school, became the second-best part of his day, and he didn't want to be late.

Jay rushed through his morning routine, and came running out of his backyard in a flurry. He saw Ava standing by her back gate and waved.

She waved back, and Jay jogged through the snow over to her.

"Jay Noble, I almost left without you," Ava said when he was close enough.

"I'm sorry…morning practice went long. It won't happen again," Jay said.

"It better not. Or I'll find someone else to walk with."

"Like who? Him?" Jay said pointing at a snowman with half its head crumbled off.

"Umm. No. I don't think we'd get very far," Ava said. "I think he's stuck there."

They both busted out laughing.

"Probably not the best walking buddy," Jay said.

"Probably not. But at least he would always be there waiting for me. Unlike you," Ava said and pushed his shoulder.

"Hey, now! It was one time. What about when he melts, huh? Then what?"

Ava grinned. "Good point."

They made it to the back of the school, and went in. As Ava and Jay walked down the hallway to class, Mr. Young, the grade seven teacher, stopped Jay in the hallway.

Mr. Young was very fit and looked like he could bench press a car. His eyes were intense and he could be intimidating to those that didn't know him. He also loved sports. His classroom was decorated with Toronto Maple Leafs and Toronto Blue Jays posters, and he coached pretty much every sport in the school.

"Your name's Jay, right?" Mr. Young said with his intense eyes locked on Jay.

"It is," Jay said cautiously. He was hoping he wasn't in trouble again for some reason.

"I've seen you outside skating on the rink before school. I wanted you to know that you are one of the most natural skaters I've ever seen."

"Thanks," Jay said, relieved.

"I'm serious. You can't teach what you can do. How long have you been playing hockey for?"

"I've never played hockey. I'm just learning how to skate this year."

"So, you don't play on a team?" Mr. Young asked.

"No. But my grandpa said I may be able to play next year."

"I think you definitely should. You're too talented not to play on a team."

"Thank you, Mr. Young."

"No problem. I look forward to teaching you next year," Mr. Young said, and he walked down the hallway to the grade seven classroom. He whistled all the way there.

"Is that what a real teacher is like?" Jay said to Ava.

"I think so…it has been a while since I've seen one," Ava replied, and they walked into their classroom.

Miss Wallace was back sitting at her desk, and scowled at them as they walked in. Standing side by side, Jay and Ava realized that as long as they were together, Miss Wallace didn't seem so scary.

But she was only back for one day, and then she was absent the whole next week, and the following week after that. During the second week, it was announced that the substitute teacher that was covering for Miss Wallace, was going to be there until the end of the school year.

Kids around the school said that Miss Wallace was fired for pulling Jay out of his desk. But Jay's mom told him that after an investigation into some of the complaints against Miss Wallace, the principal said that she went on stress leave. Either way, Jay no longer had to worry about her for the rest of the year.

CHAPTER 18

As the weather warmed up, Jay started to notice that his time on the rink would soon come to an end. He still went out there every morning, but it got to the point that the person that flooded the rink was no longer doing it. Instead, nature would have to take its course. With brown patches starting to poke through, there wasn't a lot of ice to skate on. Yet, Jay would skate around, just to get as much time on the ice as possible.

One morning, late in March, Jay and his grandpa walked to the rink only to find that there wasn't any ice left.

"So much for that, little buddy," Jay's grandpa said.

"Why couldn't it be winter all the time?" Jay asked.

Jay's grandpa laughed. "I think you're the only person in Saskatchewan that would want that."

Jay thought having winter all year long would be amazing. He could skate every single day and never have to worry about the ice melting.

"What do we do now?" Jay asked his grandpa.

"We go home, I guess."

They turned and walked back across the field.

For weeks, it felt weird for Jay not having to wake up at 6:03 a.m. each morning. Jay was able to sleep in, but he really missed those morning skates.

At school, things were much better. His substitute teacher was way nicer than Miss Wallace, Brendan and the other boys weren't able to pick on Jay as much, and there were no more trips to the principal's office. Best of all, Jay and Ava became close friends. Jay had a rough start to his first year in Saskatoon, but the rest of the school year flew by.

Jay didn't play summer hockey—or any other sport like soccer or baseball, like other kids did—but he continued to learn and practice hockey as much as he could. He still spent a lot of time shooting pucks in his grandpa's garage (but his grandma made him take down those noisy hubcaps). He also practiced stick handling on an old door that his grandpa had in the garage. He would spend hours rolling his wrists, toe dragging, and shooting off the door.

He didn't know how good he was actually getting with all that practice—no one did. But Jay was learning and developing skills all on his own. He had a dedication to learn and a work ethic that most kids his age did not have. The only downside was that he didn't have any experience playing hockey on a real team, in a real game, and wearing full equipment. But once he started doing that, he would be able to pick it up just as quickly as he learned how to skate.

Jay got his hard work and dedication from his mom. That first year in Saskatoon, Jay's mom finished her first year of law school at the top of her class. That summer she ended up getting a job in a law office so that she could make some money before the new school year started. With her new job, she was not home as much, but Jay was able to spend a lot of time with his grandma and grandpa, and his uncle Dylan came over to visit more often.

Jay was also able to spend more time with Ava. At first Ava's family wasn't too sure about Jay, especially since they were good friends with Brendan's parents. But the more they got to know Jay, they treated him like family.

Jay's first summer in Saskatoon helped him settle in, and he knew grade seven was going to be much better than the year before.

—PART 2—

GRADE SEVEN

CHAPTER 19

"Get up, it's time to go," Ava said and kicked the patio chair that Jay was lounging in.

It was a beautiful September morning—the birds were chirping, and the sun was shining right on Jay's face. He didn't move and kept his eyes closed while he soaked up the sun in Ava's backyard.

"But do I have to, mom?" Jay said.

"I am not your mom!" Ava said.

"You sure sound like it," Jay said without showing any signs that he was going to get up.

Ava went over to a green garden hose that was on the ground near by, picked it up, and pointed it at him. "If you don't get up in three seconds, I am going to spray you."

Jay opened one eye. He saw Ava holding the hose and then closed his eye again. "Good try. The water isn't even turned on."

"Fine," Ava said, and she rushed over to the water valve and turned it on all the way.

Jay heard the hose fill up with water and got up in a panic. "Okay, okay. Turn it off."

Ava kept pointing the hose at him. "Are you going to listen to me?"

"Maybe," Jay said with a grin.

"Wrong answer," she said and pulled the trigger on the nozzle but she quickly moved it downwards, so it would spray right in front of Jay's feet.

Jay jumped backwards. "You got my new shoes wet," he

whined.

"Next, I'm going to spray that new shirt of yours."

"Ava, put the hose down. Before someone gets wet," Jay said.

"The only one that will get wet is you. Now, are you going to listen to me?"

"Yes, I will do anything you want."

"That's much better," she said, and went over and turned the water off. She was still holding the hose.

Jay ran across the lawn toward the back gate. "Will you stop fooling around up there…we'll be late for our first day of grade seven."

Ava quickly turned the water back on and shot a stream into the air.

"Hey!" Jay shouted as he danced around trying to avoid the falling drops of water.

Satisfied, Ava shut the water back off, and dropped the hose.

"I barely got you," Ava said as she walked past him and opened the gate.

"Wait a second you two!" Ava's mom called out from the back door. "I want to take a picture of both of you on your first day." She walked across the backyard, and opened up the camera App on her phone. "Now scootch together and smile," Ava's mom said and held up her phone. Then she moved her head to the side. "Jay, why is your shirt all wet?"

Jay squinted his eyes and scowled at Ava. "Yeah, Ava, why is my shirt all wet?"

"I don't know what you're talking about," Ava said and beamed an innocent smile. "Can we just take the picture, please?"

Jay moved closer to Ava and smiled for the camera.

"You two look so cute," Ava's mom said, and they both started to blush. "All done. You two have a great day."

"Thanks, mom," Ava said.

"Thanks, Mrs. Berwin," Jay said.

Jay and Ava walked out into the field, and started to make their way to school.

"A picture is a good idea…selfie?" Ava said to Jay.

"Selfie," Jay said. He took out his new phone and held it up in front of them. He took one of them smiling and one of them making a silly face with their tongues out.

"Let me see," Ava said and took his phone. "Those are keepers. Send them to me."

She handed back his phone.

"On it," Jay said, and he tapped the screen a few times to send them.

Jay was so grateful to have a friend like Ava. He still remembered that feeling he got when she first left a note on his desk—those butterflies in his stomach. That feeling always returned every time he saw her since. Now that he was in grade seven, he started to think that he may like her more than a friend. But he was too scared to ever tell her that.

"I still can't believe you sprayed me with a hose," Jay said as they walked. He bent down and picked up a yellow dandelion in the middle of the soccer field, and spun the stem around in his fingers.

"You deserved it," Ava said.

"I did not."

"You did. I told you to get up, and you wouldn't listen."

"But I was having a nice rest. Plus, we didn't even need to leave yet. We're probably going to be the first ones there."

Jay ran over to the hockey rink, and looked over the boards—almost as if he was hoping there would magically be ice there. He waited for Ava to catch up, and then they kept walking.

"We won't be the first ones there," Ava said.

"Yes, we will."

"No, we won't."

"Wanna bet?" Jay said, and he paused right outside the school door.

"Sure," Ava said. "What's the wager?"

"If you win, I'll give you this dandelion," Jay said and held it out in front of him.

"Oh, how lovely. And if you win?"

"You owe me some ice cream," Jay said.

"That's not a fair bet."

"You're cranky today," Jay said. He grabbed the silver door handle and pulled it open. "You won't win this bet, so it won't even matter."

"Just go inside," Ava said, and gave Jay a shove.

"You first."

"Wow, thanks," Ava said. "That's the nicest thing you've done for me all morning."

The school had that freshly cleaned smell. The hallways were newly waxed, the walls were bright white and spotless, and everything looked perfectly in place. It looked like a new school for a new year.

Jay and Ava walked down the hall and entered the grade seven classroom. Mr. Young was sitting at his computer, and he was the only one in there.

"What did I tell you?" Jay said holding out his arms as if to present the class to Ava. "First ones here."

They both started laughing.

"What's so funny?" Mr. Young asked.

"Nothing," Jay said. "Ava just owes me an ice cream."

"Do not," Ava said.

"Do to," Jay said.

"Can we sit anywhere?" Ava asked Mr. Young

"That would be fine, as long as you don't disrupt the class," Mr. Young said.

Jay and Ava chose two desks beside each other near the window. Jay could see the rink, and his grandparent's house in the background. It was the perfect spot.

Shortly after, two of Ava's friends came and chose desks near

Ava as well. They both said "Hi" to Ava and Jay. Most of the girls in the class—especially Ava's friends—were much friendlier to Jay, now that he was friends with Ava. He no longer felt alone.

Brendan, Ryan, and Tyson came strolling in carrying their hockey sticks. Even though it was still summer weather outside, they were going to start their hockey games at recess. Jay loved hockey, but after what happened in grade six, he didn't even want to join them anymore. Besides, he had Ava to hang out with at recess.

"I was hoping he moved schools," Ava leaned over and whispered to Jay.

"Me too," Jay said.

Before class even started, Brendan and the rest of the boys had to be separated. Right from the beginning, they didn't get away with everything. Jay could tell things were going to be different this school year. But Brendan was the same old Brendan.

When the bell rang for the first recess, Jay and Ava walked to the back doors together. Brendan and his friends were about to head outside when Brendan saw Jay and Ava. "Hey, Ava," Brendan said. "I see you're still hanging out with this loser," he said pointing his stick at Jay.

"Just ignore him, Jay. Let's go," she said grabbing Jay's arm.

"You hear that, Jay? I see Ava still has to stick up for you cause you're too much of a sissy to do it yourself," Brendan said.

"Brendan Walker, that's enough! There will be none of that this year," Mr. Young said loudly as he walked into the entryway. He went right up to Brendan and towered over him. "You stay here, I want to talk to you...the rest of you go outside for recess."

For the first time since Jay had been to that school, he heard a teacher talk sternly to Brendan. It was a nice change.

Ava and Jay went out to the field and kicked a soccer ball around during recess. Some of Ava's friends joined them, and they ran around making long passes to each other. At one point, Jay looked over at the other kids playing hockey, and part of him wished he was there with them. But after what happened last year, he knew that wasn't a good idea.

Jay had a normal first day of school, and normal felt good. Jay and Ava got up to leave at the end of the day, and Mr. Young called over to Jay.

"Jay," Mr. Young said. "I need to talk to you."

What now? Jay thought. *What did Brendan say to him?*

Every time a teacher wanted to talk to him, he automatically felt like he was going to be blamed for something he didn't do. He automatically thought that Brendan was behind it.

"I'll wait for you outside," Ava said and gave him a comforting smile.

"Ava, you can stay. I'd like to talk to you, too," Mr. Young said. He put some papers down on a table at the front of the class, and then walked over to their desks. "I wanted to touch base with you two, and I wanted to ask you to please tell me any time that Brendan, or anyone else is disrespectful to you, hurts you, or anything like that. I do not want a repeat of last year."

Jay was so relieved to hear that. "Sounds good, Mr. Young. Thank you," Jay said.

"No problem," Mr. Young said. "Oh, and Jay. I noticed you weren't playing hockey with the boys at recess."

"Yeah, no. I won't be playing with them. That was a whole other thing last year."

"But do you want to? I could talk to the whole group about being respectful, including everyone, and being good team players."

"Thanks, but I'm good. I would rather hang out with Ava, anyway."

"Let me know if you ever change your mind. Are you going to tryout for a hockey team this year?"

"I'm really not sure yet. My mom says I might be able to, but I don't have any equipment or anything, and I heard it's pretty expensive."

"I hope you can. I think you'd surprise a lot of people, and even yourself at how good you would be. Let me know if there's anything I can do for you, or if you have any questions about hockey. Sound good?"

"Sounds good. Thanks, Mr. Young."

"Have a good night you two. See you tomorrow."

"See you tomorrow," Jay and Ava said.

"Mr. Young is so nice," Ava said when they got into the hallway.

"So nice! Could you imagine if he was our teacher last year instead of Miss Wallace," he said and shuttered. "My first year in Saskatoon would have been so much better."

"Speak of the devil," Ava whispered.

Miss Wallace walked out of her classroom, looked at them, squinted her eyes, looked away, and walked right by them without saying a word.

"She is a mean and unhappy lady. I wonder why she chose to be a teacher," Jay said when they got outside.

"No kidding. Why teach kids if you don't even like kids? I was hoping she would have moved schools, too," Ava said.

"Me too," Jay said.

And they both laughed.

CHAPTER 20

Before the school year started, Jay's mom told him that she was going to be much busier than she was the year before. She would be working very hard at her law classes, and she would often be at the law library on the University of Saskatchewan campus until late. For the most part, Jay's grandma and grandpa would take care of him, feed him, and make sure he would finish all of his homework. Jay was sad that he would not get to see his mom as often, but he was proud of her. He knew she always wanted to be a lawyer, and now, she was so close to becoming one.

When Jay got home from his first day of grade seven, his mom was also getting home from her first day of school. They met each other at the back door.

"Look at that perfect timing," Jay's mom said, and put her arm around his shoulder. "Just a couple of kids on their first day of school."

"You're far from a kid, mom," Jay said.

"What is that supposed to mean? Are you calling me old?"

"Maybe," Jay teased.

"You watch it, mister! I was going to tell you that I had a big surprise for you, but maybe I won't after that."

"I'm sorry, how was your first day of school, my young and pretty mom."

"That's much better," his mom laughed. "It wasn't too bad. It's a good thing I bought you that cell phone, because I think I'll be at the library more than I thought. We'll have to text each other, and Facetime so I can remember what you look like. How was your day, Jay-Jay?"

Jay laughed. "It wasn't too bad, either. My teacher is a lot nicer this year, and he already shouted at Brendan. What's this big surprise?"

"Already shouted at Brendan? Sounds like a great teacher…I shouldn't say that, but it's true. Let's go inside and I'll tell you the surprise."

Jay held the door open for his mom. "After you, young lady."

"Oh, I raised such gentleman."

Jay loved it when his mom was in a good mood, and on that day, she appeared to be in an extremely good mood.

Jay put his bag in the back closet, and kicked off his shoes.

"Surprise time!" Jay said.

"Be patient. Let me put my things away."

"I don't want to be patient. You're the one that brought up the idea of a surprise."

Jay's mom seemed to be moving in slow motion on purpose. She slowly untied her shoes. Took them off. Carefully placed them in the closet. Jay couldn't stand it.

"What are you a sloth!" Jay said.

His mom giggled.

"What's all the commotion about," Jay's grandma said coming out of the kitchen.

"Mom said she had a big surprise for me, and now she's moving at a snail's pace, and won't tell me."

Right then, Jay heard his uncle Dylan and grandpa's voice coming up the stairs from the basement.

"It should be all there," Jay heard his uncle Dylan say. Uncle Dylan emerged from the stairway carrying a large hockey bag.

"Unc, I didn't know you were here. What's with the hockey bag?"

"Hey, buddy," Uncle Dylan said to Jay. "Can I tell him?" Uncle Dylan looked at Jay's mom.

Jay's mom nodded. "Go ahead."

"Tell me what?" Jay asked.

"Well, I'm carrying this hockey bag for you. It's a full set of equipment we put together. How would you like to play hockey this year?" Uncle Dylan said, and tossed down the hockey bag. It made a loud thump when it hit the floor.

"That would be awesome!" Jay said.

"And that's the big surprise. Your grandpa signed you up. Tryouts are happening already in a couple weeks," Jay's mom said.

"Thanks, mom!" Jay said and ran over to the hockey bag.

"Don't just thank me," his mom said. "It was mostly your grandpa's idea. He said you are more than ready to be on a team."

"Thanks, grandpa!"

"You're welcome, little buddy. You can thank Uncle Dylan too. He bought you a new hockey bag, and a few pieces of equipment. The rest are some of his old stuff that's still in good shape."

"Thanks, Unc!" Jay said. He felt like a thanking machine.

"No problem, pal," Uncle Dylan said. "Now let's open up the bag and see if everything fits."

Jay unzipped his new hockey bag, and riffled through it. There was a combination of old and new equipment, but that didn't bother him one bit. To him, everything was brand new. He was simply so excited that he was going to get to play real hockey on a team.

"Here, let's take it to the living room, so we have more space," Uncle Dylan said.

Jay picked up the bag, and hauled it to the living room. He took everything out, and Uncle Dylan explained what each piece of equipment was, and where it went. Then, Uncle Dylan helped Jay try it all on.

Once Jay was all suited up, he felt like he was ready for battle.

Jay's mom walked into the living room and took a look at her son. "Now you look like a hockey player, Jay-Jay. How does it all fit?"

"Pretty much everything fits," Uncle Dylan replied for him. "We tried to put on the skates he used last year, but he could barely get his foot in. The next size are my CCMs and they seem to fit perfect. He must have had a big growth spurt like me."

"That's great!" his mom said. "And he has been growing like a weed."

"Must be all the perogies grandma feeds him," Uncle Dylan said and chuckled. "The biggest thing is that he will need a new helmet. They have different regulations now than they did when I played. Oh, and I almost forgot, and it's the most important thing. We will need to get him some new jock shorts and a cup. He definitely doesn't want to wear my old sweaty ones."

"Gross. Definitely not," Jay's mom said and laughed with a scrunched-up face.

"Should we go to the sports store before supper?" Uncle Dylan asked.

"Can we mom?" Jay added.

"That's fine with me," his mom said.

Jay got out of his equipment, and him and his uncle headed off to the sports store.

Jay walked into the store with his uncle and came to a stop. He looked around and was in awe of all the equipment. He thought his grandma and grandpa's storage room was amazing, but this was unlike anything he had ever seen before. There were rows and rows of packed shelves full of all types of sports equipment. Sports equipment also hung from every wall.

"Welcome to one of my favourite places in the city," Uncle Dylan said. "Beautiful, isn't it?"

"It sure is," Jay said as he took it all in.

"So, let's do this. Hockey equipment is over there," Uncle Dylan said gesturing to the back of the store.

Jay could hear the grinding noise of skates being sharpened as they headed in that direction. Down one of the rows he let his fingertips drag over all the composite hockey sticks as he followed his uncle.

"Check these out," Uncle Dylan said handing Jay a skate. "It's lighter than a pair of socks. Smells better, too."

Jay held it in his hand and moved it up and down to test its weight. He didn't understand how something could be so light.

"Smell it," his uncle said.

"I'm not going to smell it."

"Just do it."

"No!"

"Do it!"

"Fine," Jay said. He held the skate to his nose and took a sniff. It smelled like the rest of the store—like new sports equipment.

Uncle Dylan laughed. "And? Does it smell better than a pair of socks?"

"Maybe yours. Mine smell great."

"Get out of here," Uncle Dylan said playfully swiping at Jay's shoulder.

Jay handed the skate back to his uncle and watched him put it back in its spot on a wall filled with skates. Jay noticed the price tag: $950. Jay could only dream of owning skates like that.

They eventually made it to the helmets, and a worker there helped Jay try a few on. Every time Jay put a helmet on, it felt strange—he wasn't used to having a piece of plastic and foam shoved onto his head. And when they did up the straps of the black cage, for some reason, he felt trapped. He never wore a helmet when he skated on the outdoor rink, and he now appreciated the freedom.

When they finally found the right one that fit, Uncle Dylan slapped Jay in the helmet a few times. "Does that hurt?"

"No." Jay laughed.

"Perfect. That means it works."

Jay took the helmet off, and they put it back in the box.

As they walked to the front of the store, Uncle Dylan took a package from a hook, and tossed it to Jay. "Now you're all set, Neph."

Jay caught it and looked at it. It was his new jock shorts. He was glad he didn't have to try it on. Uncle Dylan bought him his last two pieces of equipment, and they headed back home. Jay had all the equipment he needed, and he was one step closer to being ready for tryouts.

Before supper, Jay dressed and undressed in his hockey equipment several times in the living room of his grandma and grandpa's house. When he was confident enough on how to put it all on, and knew where the tape went on his socks (like Uncle Dylan showed him), Jay walked around the house. He even sat and ate supper in his equipment. His family teased him, but he wanted to get used to all that equipment that he had never worn before. Skating, stick handling, and shooting on an outdoor rink with winter clothes on, was a lot different than skating, stick handling, and shooting with full hockey gear on. Then he went outside, in his full gear—without his skates of course—and practiced stick handling and shooting in the garage.

That night, he probably would have slept in his equipment, but that's where his mom drew the line. But tryouts were only two weeks away, and Jay wanted to be ready.

CHAPTER 21

On the way to the hockey rink, Jay was both excited and nervous for his very first hockey tryout. He looked out the window while his grandpa drove. Jay felt that he was ready to show up and do his best, but he didn't know exactly how he would match up against other players his age. He always practiced on his own, and he knew he was getting better, but he didn't know if he was good enough to play on a real team. He knew the basic skills, but he didn't know the rules, or how to play any specific position. He would have to learn as he went.

When Jay pushed the heavy door to the dressing room with his shoulder, the smell of old hockey sweat hit him like a body check. He didn't think that smell was normal, and would have turned around and left, but a group of boys were already in there. That awful smell didn't seem to bother them.

Jay looked around the room and the only person he recognized was Brendan. They made eye contact.

"What on earth are you doing here?" Brendan said welcoming Jay.

Jay knew that he would probably see Brendan at some point on the ice, but he was hoping that he would be in a different dressing room than him. "What does it look like. I'm here to try out," Jay said and threw down his bag as far away as possible from Brendan. But in a small hockey dressing room, that would never be far enough.

"You don't know how to play hockey...but whatever, you're going to get cut anyway," Brendan said.

That didn't bother Jay at all. He didn't care if he didn't make the highest tier. All he wanted to do was play hockey.

Jay got dressed like he practiced several times at home, and he tried his best to ignore Brendan's comments. The whole time Jay was getting ready, Brendan said things like: *"Look at Jay's shin pads, they look like they are a hundred years old; look at his skates, I bet he can't even skate in those things; look at his gloves, they don't even make those anymore,"* and on it went. Jay didn't understand why Brendan paid so much attention to him. If someone doesn't like someone else, why would someone focus on that person every chance they got? It was all very strange to Jay. Finally, Jay got fed up, and said, "Stop staring at me while I get dressed, you creep," and that actually shut Brendan up—at least until they got on the ice.

When Jay stepped out onto the ice, he did his best to try and follow what the other players did. He skated around the ice and took mental notes. He saw that some players were skating around the rink, stick handling the puck, and shooting on the goalie at one end. They would then find another puck, and do the same thing towards the other end of the ice. He also saw Brendan trying to take the puck away from people skating by, and even tripping them, and then laughing. Jay realized that Brendan was a jerk everywhere he went.

As Jay skated around, he couldn't believe how smooth the ice was. He actually had to take off his glove, reach down, and touch it. He felt the cold, smooth surface on his palm and put his glove back on. Even after a fresh flood, the outdoor rink he skated on never came close to being that smooth—it was bumpy, snowy, and had deep cuts made by tight turns.

Jay circled around and picked up a puck, but it immediately got away from him. He found out that the puck moved a lot faster than what he was used to. But that only meant his shot would be harder, too. He just had to adapt.

When Jay was skating to pick up another puck, a coach blew a whistle, and Jay followed all the other players to the middle of the ice.

"Alright, gentleman, take a knee," the coach said and all the players instantly got down on one knee. The coach was wearing all black—from his skates to his helmet. Jay thought he looked like a shadow. "My name is Coach Steven, and to the right of me is Coach Paul, and standing by the boards to my left over there is Coach Brian. We want to welcome everyone to this year's U13 tryouts. I see many of you have grown over the summer, and I'm looking forward to another great hockey season. Just like last year, you will have two skill-session evaluations, and then scrimmages will start, and we hope to have all teams picked within a couple weeks. I wish everybody luck, and do your best out there...Brendan would you like to lead everyone in a warm-up stretch."

A lot of what the coach was saying didn't make a lot of sense to Jay. He didn't know where he would end up, and he didn't know much about tryouts to begin with. It didn't really matter to him, as long as he was playing hockey.

When the coach stopped talking, all the players got to their skates, got in a circle around Brendan, and dropped to the ice. Then they followed what Brendan was doing. Jay hadn't done a lot of those stretches before, and some of them were tough for him to keep his balance on the smooth ice.

When the skill-based drills started, Jay realized he actually lucked out. Since he was new, he had a high number pinned to his jersey, and everything they did was in order. He was able to watch all the other kids perform the drills, and this gave him some time to learn what to do. Many players made everything look so easy, but he took comfort in realizing that some weren't that strong. He quickly realized, that with all his practicing, he was a much better skater, stick-handler, and shooter than many players out there.

The major downside was that Brendan was number 1, so every time he finished a drill, he would end up at the back of the line right behind Jay.

The first drill was a simple skating and puck-handling drill. They had to start in one corner at one end of the ice and skate around the five large circles down to the other end. Jay watched all the other players do it until it was his turn.

"Hey, loser, don't blow it," Brendan said right before Jay took off.

Jay lost the puck on the very first circle and he heard Brendan laugh. That smooth surface was still hard to get used to. But back in the lineup at the other end, he practiced stick handling while he waited for his next turn.

Jay was able to start the drill before Brendan made it back down the ice this time, and he was able to perform the drill perfectly. When they finished the drill, they were all able to go grab some water, and then the next drill was explained.

The next drill was the easiest—it was the speed test. They had to skate from the goal line, all the way down to the other end, slap the boards with their stick, and skate all the way back across the goal line where they started. Three skaters would line up on the goal line, and they would race against each other, but the evaluators were timing each skater individually. Since it was all done by the number on their jerseys, some players were grouped with others and were completely mismatched. Some would already be slapping the boards on the other end, while the other players were just crossing the second blue line. The way the numbers worked out, Jay was paired up with the player before him, and there wasn't a third skater.

Brendan decided to jump in there and race again. "Watch and learn, loser," Brendan said to Jay and lined up beside him. Everyone knew that Brendan was the fastest skater in the Renegade zone—he had been the last few years. Jay lined up in the middle of the ice on the goal line. The coach blew the whistle, and Jay took off and skated as hard as he could—just like he did on all those early mornings before school. To everyone's surprise—coaches and everyone watching—Jay led the two skaters by several strides. He was the first one to smack the boards, and his lead grew even more as he headed back down the ice. He easily crossed the goal line before the other two.

"Hey, Brendan," Jay said. "I thought you were fast."

"I wasn't trying," Brendan said nonchalant. "I'll destroy you next time."

"We'll see about that," Jay said. He knew that he shocked Brendan, and it felt good. It felt really good.

The next drill was the backwards skating speed test. This test was the exact same, but it had to be done skating backwards. Once again Jay was paired up with one other player, and Brendan jumped up to race him another time. Brendan didn't say a word.

When the coach blew the whistle, they took off. Jay started off doing crossovers to get started, and then he did quick and hard "C" cuts all the way down the ice. Just like before, he was ahead of the other two. He snow-plowed as he approached the boards, stopped, slapped the boards, started with several crossovers, and he made hard "C" cuts on the way back, with a few cross overs here and there. He was able to watch Brendan struggle to keep up, but it was no use. He beat Brendan and the other player by a huge amount. Everyone in the rink was amazed.

"Let me guess, you weren't trying again?" Jay said to Brendan.

"Shut up," Brendan said hunched over.

Jay's skating was definitely the best part of his game. For the rest of the tryout, he didn't out-perform Brendan in much else. But Jay was better than many others. He was also the type of kid that would learn things instantaneously, and he had a lot of potential.

In the dressing room after the tryout, some of the players asked where Jay had learned how to skate so fast. Jay shrugged his shoulders and smiled.

"Hey, Brendan," Ryan Fitzgerald said. "How does it feel to not be the fastest player in our zone anymore?"

"Shut up, Fitz. I'm still the fastest," Brendan said. "I wasn't trying. I'm automatically going to make A, anyway. I don't even have to go to these stupid tryouts."

"Jay sure is fast though," Ryan said.

"He's not that fast. Plus, he sucks at everything else," Brendan said, and sprayed water from his water bottle into his mouth.

"He didn't look too bad to me," a second-year player named Blake, said.

The boys had this conversation in the dressing room in front of Jay, and he didn't say a word. He sat there and enjoyed having some of the other players speak up for him. It was much better to have others talk about his skating, than him talking about it himself.

When Jay finished getting out of his equipment and back into his clothes, he got up and lifted his hockey bag over his shoulder. Just as he did, Brendan came over and sprayed water all over his face and hair. Jay tried to cover his head with his arms. "Get out of here!" Jay yelled.

Brendan stopped and laughed. A lot of the other players laughed as well. Jay was angry, wet, and wanted to get out of there. As he left the dressing room, he started to have second thoughts about if he actually wanted to play on a team.

"Jay Noble?" Coach Steven said as Jay got out of the dressing room. Before Jay could say anything, the coach continued. "I'm Coach Steven, I just wanted to say that you played really well out there today, and I wanted to know where you played hockey last year?"

"I didn't play hockey last year…this is my first year," Jay said.

"Your first year? Like in Saskatoon?" Coach Steven asked, confused. He didn't think it was possible that this kid could be playing hockey for the first time.

"Well, yes. It's my first year in Saskatoon. But it is also my first year playing hockey. I just started to learn how to skate last year."

"No kidding?" Coach Steven said, still not sure if he was hearing Jay correctly, or simply misunderstanding. "Great job today. And good luck with the rest of your tryouts."

"Thanks, coach," Jay replied and walked to where his grandpa was standing.

"Great work today, little buddy," his grandpa said, "and look at all that sweat. It's practically pouring off of you."

"It's mostly water. Brendan sprayed me with his water bottle."

"Is that what you were talking to his dad about?" Jay's grandpa asked.

"His dad?" Jay said.

"The coach you were just talking to. That's Brendan's dad," his grandpa said.

Jay looked back to where Coach Steven was standing. Then he turned and started to walk towards the door with his grandpa. "No, he said I did a great job out there, and he wanted to know where I played hockey last year."

"What did he say when you said this was your first year?" his grandpa asked.

"He looked a little confused," Jay replied.

"I don't think a lot of people will believe you when you tell them that you haven't played before. You were one of the best players out there, Jay. And you were by far the fastest. A lot of parents were talking about you," Jay's grandpa said, and held the outside door so Jay could maneuver through.

"Really? What were they saying?" Jay said, and readjusted his hockey bag on his shoulder.

"They were amazed at how fast you were, and they wanted to know where you came from."

"Did you tell them?"

"No. They will figure it out eventually," Jay's grandpa said with a smile.

Jay didn't know what his grandpa meant by that, and he didn't know why he smiled. "Grandpa, do you think Brendan's dad knew who I was?"

"It doesn't sound like it. But he will find out soon enough, too," Jay's grandpa said.

Jay threw his hockey bag in his grandpa's trunk, but immediately couldn't wait to get back on the ice again.

CHAPTER 22

Two nights later, Jay had his second skills tryout. He was more comfortable out there than the first one. He knew what to expect, and he knew the drills. If others weren't impressed by Jay after the first tryout, they were blown away by the second one. What Jay didn't realize, was that the evaluators scored him in the top five ranking in skills.

Jay's first two tryouts went better than he could have possibly imagined—it went better than anyone could have possibly imagined. Who would have ever thought that a kid with no experience could be better than most of the other kids out there? Some would chalk it up to natural talent, but that's because they didn't see all the hard work and dedication. They didn't see all of the early morning practices. Either way, some would say that this kid was meant to play hockey.

The next night was the scrimmage portion of the tryout. Jay was looking forward to getting out there and practicing all of his skills in a game setting for the first time. Most kids didn't enjoy tryouts, but Jay was different. He always wanted to learn, and wanted to be on the ice no matter what.

When Jay got to the hockey rink, he found his name on a list that was posted to the dressing room door. Jay scanned the list, and sure enough, he was on the same team as Brendan. He took a deep breath, and pushed open the door. When he walked in, he was greeted with, "Hey, look, the loser is here."

Jay pretended he didn't hear Brendan, and put his bag down, and took a seat. Brendan continued to make rude comments towards him, but Jay got ready in silence. Jay knew that it was going to be difficult to play on the same team as Brendan, but he only had to suffer through it for one or two scrimmages. Jay felt like he could handle that.

Before Jay was about to put on his skates, Brendan left the dressing room, and came back in. "Hey, loser. There's some weird old guy looking for you," Brendan said, and threw a ball of sock tape towards Jay.

"Just leave me alone," Jay said.

"So, you're not going to go? I think the weird old guy is your grandpa. He said it was an emergency or something."

"What? Really?"

"You better go see for yourself," Brendan said.

Jay put on his shoes and walked out of the dressing room half-dressed in hockey equipment. His grandpa wasn't out there. Jay walked down the hallway, and still did not see his grandpa. He was concerned about what the emergency was, but then he realized that Brendan was most likely lying.

Jay went back into the dressing room and Brendan was over top of Jay's bag, and he stood up swiftly.

"What are you doing with my stuff?" Jay hollered.

"Nothing, loser. I was getting my ball of sock tape you stole from me," Brendan said.

"Stole your ball of sock tape? You threw it at me."

"Whatever, loser. You better not suck out there today. We want to win."

Jay looked through his equipment to see what Brendan was actually doing. He thought he was probably going to take something so he couldn't play, or mess with him in some way. But all his equipment was there. Then Jay saw that one of his skates was on top of his bag, and he hadn't brought them out of the side pocket yet. He looked inside, tipped it upside-down, and tried to figure out what Brendan had done to it. Some of the boys— including Brendan—seemed to be watching him. Jay was suspicious, but everything looked normal, and he continued to get fully dressed in his hockey equipment.

When it was time to go on the ice, Jay walked out with the rest of the team. He stepped onto the ice with his left skate, and then the right, and the second his right skate made contact with the ice, it slid from under him, and he fell forward awkwardly on his knees. It felt like his blade was covered in something, and it couldn't dig in to the ice. Brendan skated over, stopped right in front of Jay, and sprayed him with snow. "What's wrong, loser, can't skate?" he said, laughed, and then skated away.

Jay tried to stand up, and again, his right skate slid from under him. He sat down and tried to look at the blade of his skate, but it wasn't easy to see with all that equipment on. He tried to stand up again and fell. That's when it hit him—Brendan must have done something to his skate blade. He was too busy looking inside his skate, thinking Brendan put something in there, that he didn't think of checking the blade. Jay managed to pull himself up against the boards, and he stood there holding on like he was on the edge of a cliff.

"Hey, Jay, you should be skating around and getting warmed up before the scrimmage starts," Coach Brian said as he stepped on the ice.

"I can't. There's something wrong with my skate," Jay said.

"Let me take a look," Coach Brian said pulling off his hockey gloves. He got on his knee and had Jay lift his right skate. Coach Brian looked at the blade carefully, and rubbed his thumb along the blade. "Jay, you didn't happen to walk on concrete or something since last tryout, did you?"

"No. They have been in my bag since—" Jay stopped himself. "It was Brendan. He did something to them."

"Brendan Walker?" Coach Brian said. Then he stood up, and put his hockey gloves back on.

"Yeah. He told me there was an emergency, and my grandpa needed to see me. I left the dressing room for a minute, and when

I got back, Brendan was over top of my hockey bag."

"I don't think he would do something like that," Coach Brian said.

"Yes, he would. He picks on me at school all the time."

"All right, well, let me help you to the dressing room. I'll try to get this sorted out."

Coach Brian helped Jay off the ice, and Jay went back to the dressing room. When he got there, he sat down over his hockey bag, and a huge lump formed in his throat. All he wanted to do was play hockey, and now he had to miss his tryout because a bully would not leave him alone.

Jay's grandpa came in the dressing room, and looked at Jay concerned. "What's wrong, little buddy?"

"Brendan did something to my skate. It has a whole bunch of nicks on the blade. I can't skate. I can't tryout. And I have to go home."

"Let me see," Jay's grandpa said. He rubbed his thumb along the blade. "This blade is ruined. He did this?"

All Jay could do was nod his head.

Jay's grandpa was about to say something he didn't want to say in front of Jay, but Brendan and Coach Steven came in.

"Take off your skates," Coach Steven said firmly to Brendan.

"But I didn't do anything," Brendan complained.

"That's enough. Taylor admitted to his dad that you did it."

"Jay, I'm deeply sorry for what my son did. What size of skates are you?" Coach Steven said.

"Mine are a four," Jay replied.

"Brendan's are a five and half. I know they may be a little big, and they're not your own, but they are brand new, and you can give them a try today."

"But dad, those are mine. What will I wear?" Brendan whined.

"You are going to sit and watch today, and think about what you did. Your actions are completely unacceptable, and that is not how you behave as a teammate," Coach Steven said.

"He's not my teammate," Brendan said under his breath.

"He is today. And you two might be teammates in the near future, too," Coach Steven said.

Jay sat there stunned. He had never seen anyone talk like that to Brendan. Coach Steven made Brendan take off his skates and walk them over to Jay and hand them to him. Brendan didn't make eye contact with Jay, but with his father's command, he muttered a forced but reluctant, "Sorry," as he handed over the skates.

When Jay grabbed the skates, he recognized them right away—these were the $950 skates that him and his uncle saw at the sports store. He wasn't going to smell them this time, though.

Jay put them on and tied them up tight. When he stood up, there was room near the toes, but he found that they fit better than he thought they would. He was going to enjoy every minute of wearing Brendan's skates.

"This isn't fair," Brendan said to his dad as Jay stood up to head to the ice.

"Fair? Was damaging Jay's skate fair so that he had to sit out?" Coach Steven said.

Brendan put his head down and looked at the ground.

"That's what I thought," Coach Steven said to Brendan. "Now let's go Jay, we need to start our scrimmage."

"Remember, just do your best and have fun," Jay's grandpa said, and patted Jay on the shoulder pads.

It took Jay's grandpa everything within him not to say something to Brendan on the way out, but he had to remind himself that Brendan was only a kid. Even if he was an awful kid at that. Jay's grandpa walked out of the dressing room to watch his grandson play.

When Jay stepped out onto the ice, he glided effortlessly, and realized it felt strange as he took several strides. These skates were so light and he barely felt them on his feet. Jay was happy as long as he was able to skate, but this was different. This was nice. If he had these skates while racing Brendan again, he would have beat him by even more.

Coach Steven blew the whistle, and each team gathered up the pucks, and headed to their bench. Jay barely had a chance to warm up, but he was ready to go.

Coach Brian put Jay up with the forwards and he told him he was playing right wing. All Jay knew about that position was what he had seen on TV. But as always, he watched the players who were out on the ice closely, and he was a quick learner.

Without Brendan being out there, it was clear that Jay was the smoothest and fastest skater each time he stepped on the ice. The coaches and evaluators observed that his positioning and passing were off, but that didn't matter as much. That could be taught. That could be practiced.

Every time Jay touched the puck, something special would happen. It didn't take him long to realize that he could simply skate right past most players. Jay ended up scoring five goals in that first scrimmage. But what coaches liked the most, was the fact that he skated hard and tried to get the puck back every time the other team had it. For those that were watching, when he was out there, it's like he never stopped skating.

In the dressing room after the scrimmage—since Brendan wasn't in there—no one said anything bad to Jay. Considering how the tryout started, he walked out from the dressing room feeling good with the way he played. He had a lot of fun out there. Jay walked over to Coach Steven and handed him Brendan's skates.

"Jay, I'm sorry for what my son did to you today," Coach Steven said. "And I'm sorry for anything else he has done at school. I don't know why he is like that. I'll keep on him to try to make him be better. You're a good kid, Jay, and a great hockey player."

"Thanks, Coach," Jay said, and he smiled all the way over to his grandpa.

CHAPTER 23

"How was your tryout last night," Ava asked Jay on their daily walk to school.

"It was good, but pretty crazy," he replied. He noticed Ava was about to step into a gopher hole and gently pulled her towards him. "Watch out!"

"Yikes, that was a close one!" Ava said as she avoided the hole. "What do you mean crazy?"

"Brendan wrecked one of my skate blades before the scrimmage, and his dad made him take off his skates, and give them to me."

Ava stopped and looked at Jay. "Let me get this straight, you used Brendan's skates for the whole tryout?

"I did."

"What did he use?" she asked with raised eyebrows.

"Nothing, his dad made him watch."

Ava laughed. "That is the best thing I have ever heard," she said in between laughs. "I could just picture him now. He was probably so angry. Oh, that is great."

They both kept on walking.

"It was pretty great. But now I have to get my skate fixed before tomorrow night. I have another scrimmage," Jay said.

"That sucks. How did he wreck it?"

"I don't know. He tricked me to get me out of the dressing room, and then he must have grinded my skate blade with something."

"He's such a jerk. Hey, I can ask my brother Tyler if he has any old skates your size…just in case you can't get yours fixed in time."

"That would be awesome…thanks."

"Anytime," Ava said.

Jay reached the door first, opened it, and held it there for Ava to pass through. "What I'd like to do is wear Brendan's again. They were so nice."

"I bet. He has always been spoiled."

They walked down the hallway to their classroom and Mr. Young was already in there like he always was. He turned from where he was writing on the whiteboard and greeted them. "Good morning, you two."

"Good morning, Mr. Young," they both said at the same time and walked to their desks.

"Jay, I heard about you last night," Mr. Young said, and put the cap on the blue marker he was using.

"Really? How?" Jay asked.

"I'm coaching a U18 hockey team, and I was at the rink last night and some of the other coaches I know were talking about this unbelievable Jay Noble kid. They wanted to know where he came from and if it was true that he had never played hockey before."

"That's pretty cool," Jay said. "Did you say anything to them?"

"I told them that I teach a Jay Noble and he is one of the best skaters I've ever seen, and that it was true, this is his first year playing hockey. They were all very impressed. I think you're starting to become some sort of legend."

"You should tell Mr. Young what Brendan did before tryouts," Ava said.

"What did Brendan do?"

"It was nothing," Jay said and shook his head.

"You see, you'll be a strong leader someday, Jay. Even when people mistreat you, you hardly complain. You just take everything in stride," Mr. Young said. "I already heard about the skates."

Two other students walked in and Mr. Young greeted them.

Jay looked over at Ava and she was resting her cheek in her hand and smiling at him. "What?" Jay asked with a smirk.

"Nothing," Ava replied. "I'm just looking at Jay the legend."

Jay shook his head and smiled.

A few minutes later, Brendan and Ryan showed up to class. Brendan didn't even look in Jay's direction. In fact, he avoided Jay all day. *He must have got in big trouble from his dad*, Jay thought. For the first time in a while, Jay was able to have an uneventful day.

CHAPTER 24

Jay's grandpa wasn't able to get Jay's skate repaired. Luckily, Ava was there to save the day again. Her brother, Tyler, had a pair of skates that fit Jay perfectly, and they were much newer than his uncle Dylan's skates. Tyler told Jay that if he liked the skates, he could keep them. Either way, Jay didn't have a choice—he had his second scrimmage that night.

That second scrimmage went way smoother than the one before. First off, Jay was relieved to find out that Brendan was on the other team for the second scrimmage—that meant he did not have to share the same dressing room as him. Secondly, on the ice, Jay was playing right wing once again, but his grandpa and Uncle Dylan gave him some tips, and they watched some videos on how to play the position. He didn't feel as out of place this time around. Lastly, and most of all, with all the compliments he received after last scrimmage, Jay started to feel like a hockey player.

The second the puck dropped, the scrimmage became the Brendan and Jay show. Each time one of them were on the ice, all eyes were on them. They skated harder and faster than anyone else. Brendan was captain of the A team last season, and his dad was the coach, so he knew he already made the team. Jay knew Brendan was only playing that hard to show off and prove he was better than Jay. But Jay wasn't going to make it easy on him. When Brendan scored a goal, Jay went out and scored one his next shift. When Brendan made a nice play, Jay made a nicer play. Back and forth they were out there trying to one-up the other until the scrimmage was over. The big difference was that Brendan was out there frustrated and Jay was out there having fun.

With that talent, if both of them could play on the same team, they could win championships.

CHAPTER 25

A few nights later, Jay was on the driveway shooting pucks when his mom came outside with her phone. "Jay, phone is for you," she said, and reached out to give it to him.

Jay grabbed the phone and his mom took a step back and watched him with a smile on her face.

"Who is it?" Jay asked his mom.

"Answer it and find out," she whispered.

"Hello?" Jay said.

"Hey, Jay, this is Coach Steven calling from the Renegades A hockey team. How are you doing?"

"I'm good. I'm just shooting pucks on my driveway right now."

"That's what I like to hear. Anyway, I don't want to keep you too long. I am calling to congratulate you on your excellent performance at tryouts, and I want to personally welcome you to the team."

"Does that mean I made A?" Jay said surprised.

"It sure does. We are hoping to have a very successful year this year, and we believe that you will play a big role in helping us do that."

Jay didn't know what to say.

"Jay, are you there?"

"Sorry, coach. Yes, I am. I am just a little surprised. I didn't think I would make A." Then it hit him. He would be on the same team as Brendan. He didn't know if he could handle being bullied at school and outside of school all year. "Coach, do you think it's a good idea…for, you know, me to be on the same team as your son?"

"In A, we want the best players. You are far too talented not to play A. As for my son, I have already talked to him about this, and you have my personal guarantee that he won't bother you anymore. And if he does, at school or at hockey, let me know as soon as possible, and I will handle it."

"Thanks, coach."

"Anytime. Well, I have a few more phone calls to make. We have our first practice on Thursday night at six-fifteen at Archibald arena. We'll see you then."

"See you then, coach," Jay said and hung up the phone and handed it back to his mom.

"So?" Jay's mom said.

"I guess I made A," Jay said and he was still trying to process everything.

"Jay-Jay," his mom said with tears in her eyes. "I am so, so proud of you." She hugged him and held him tight. With all that Jay had been through in the last year, she thought she had made a big mistake moving back to Saskatoon and going back to school. But things were getting better, and she had tears of joy tonight, knowing that her son was a special hockey player. She knew he was going to be great at anything he tried, no matter what or who tried to stop him. She was in awe of her son. "We better go inside and tell your grandma and grandpa," she said and let go of him.

Jay's grandpa and grandma were waiting for him in the living room. Jay walked in beside his mom. "I made the A team," Jay announced.

"I knew you would," Jay's grandpa said, and he got up and put his arm around his grandson.

"Congratulations, Jay!" his grandma said and pulled him away from his grandpa and wrapped Jay up in her arms.

"Look at you, my son the hockey star!" Jay's mom said smiling.

"I'm going to go call Uncle Dylan," Jay said and broke free from his grandma.

"He'll be so excited for you!" Jay's mom said.

Jay went up into his room and got his phone to call his uncle Dylan. He looked out the window at the rink while he called.

"Jay! What's up, little bro?" Uncle Dylan answered.

"Hey, Uncle Dylan, guess what?"

"Hmm, let me think. No! It can't be! You broke my perogy eating record, didn't you?"

Jay laughed. "No, not yet. It's better than that. I made the A team for hockey."

"Yes! That is unreal! I knew you would. I'm so proud of you."

"Thanks, Unc."

"By the way, I think you broke a record that won't be beat for a long time...if ever."

"What record is that?" Jay asked.

"I think you are the only player in the history of hockey that used three different pairs of skates for their tryouts. Just so you know for next year, you are supposed to be trying out for a team, and not trying out skates."

Jay started laughing. "It wasn't my fault."

"I know that, I'm just bugging you. How were Tyler's skates?"

"I like them. They fit perfectly and he said I could keep them."

"That's awesome."

"Sure is! Anyway, I better go. I just wanted to tell you that I made the team."

"I'm proud of you, buddy. Have a good night, and I'll see you sometime this week."

"Sounds good, see-ya later."

"Later."

Jay hung up the phone, tossed it on his bed, and continued to look out the window. It was a beautiful September night, and it felt like ages ago that he stepped on that outdoor rink for the first time. Now he was officially a hockey player.

Then he realized that he had one more person he needed to tell. He picked up his phone and texted Ava:

Want to come over? I have big news.

I'll be right over! Ava sent back.

Jay went downstairs and told his mom that Ava was coming over and that he was going to go wait for her outside.

"I made some pumpkin pie," his grandma said. "Tell Ava to come in and have a piece."

"Pumpkin pie! I'll let her know," Jay said to his grandma, and went outside.

Jay grabbed his hockey stick that was on top of the hockey net on the driveway. He toe-dragged a tennis ball out of the net and shot it under the bar. He did this a few times before he saw Ava walking up the sidewalk.

"So, what's this big news?" Ava said when she got to the bottom of the driveway. She was wearing black shorts, a white t-shirt, and a Toronto Blue Jays hat with a ponytail out the back. Her family was probably watching the Blue Jays game—which they did a lot.

"My grandma made pumpkin pie!"

"Yummy!"

"Okay, that's it…that's all I wanted to tell you. You can go home now," Jay said.

"I don't think so, jerk! I'm going in that house and getting a piece of pie. Your grandma loves me and would probably give me the whole thing if I asked."

"She probably would. I have some other news, too. I made the A team for hockey."

"Jay, that's so great!" she squealed, gave him a quick hug, and pushed him away to look at him. "I knew you would! My family is going to be so happy for you. Wait, does that mean you'll be on—"

"Brendan's team?" Jay finished her thought. "Yeah, it sure does."

"Yikes. Maybe he'll change now that you are teammates."

"I was thinking the same thing. His dad is the coach, and actually seems nice, which is weird. But maybe he'll stop his son from picking on me."

"Mr. Walker is really nice. It's Mrs. Walker that Brendan probably gets it from…I mean she's nice enough to us, but she's also kind of bossy."

"Really? I've never met her, but she is the one that tried to make me pay for Brendan's stick."

"Exactly. And they didn't need the money. They have plenty of it. Anyway, enough about them. It's pie time."

Jay laughed. "Sounds good. Let's go inside."

While inside, Ava, Jay, his mom, grandma, and grandpa all sat around talking, laughing, and eating the most delicious pie in the world. Life in Saskatoon was pretty good.

CHAPTER 26

"Good morning you two, and congratulations on making the team, Jay," Mr. Young said when Jay and Ava entered the classroom the next morning.

"Do you know everything?" Ava asked.

Mr. Young laughed. "Not even close. But I do know a lot about hockey."

"Seriously, though, how did you know already? I just got called last night," Jay said.

"Jay, the day you told me you were trying out, I knew you would make the team. I could tell you were good enough after that first time I saw you skating out on the rink before school last year," Mr. Young said with a grin and walked over to his computer.

"If he saw you on the morning that I watched you out there for the first time, he definitely wouldn't be saying the same thing," Ava said to Jay.

"Ouch," Jay said and he put his hand on his chest where his heart is and acted hurt. He then slumped over on his desk.

"I'm kidding," Ava said. "But you were pretty bad."

Jay straightened up and was alive again. "Yeah, you got me there. I was awful."

"Do you think Brendan is going to say anything today about you making the team?" Ava asked.

"Who knows. We'll just have to wait and find out."

"You know what you should do? When he walks in, you should jump out of your desk, go up to him and be like

'Teammate!' and hold out your fist for a fist bump," Ava said excitedly.

"He would probably punch me right in the face if I did that."

"Yeah, he probably would. Don't do that. I like your face. Maybe you could give him a hug?"

"Okay, Ava, enough. You are being ridiculous."

"What? Everybody needs a hug sometimes."

"Do you need a hug, Ava?"

"Yes, as a matter of fact, I do."

"Fine, I will get Brendan to hug you when he gets here," Jay said.

"Gross!" Ava groaned.

"You deserved that."

Jay and Ava went back and forth teasing each other like that for a few minutes. Mr. Young sat at his desk listening to them and was shaking his head. After a while, he spoke up. "I have a quick question. I know you both live super close to the school, so why do you both come here so early before everyone else?"

"I'm not sure," Jay said.

"I have no idea," Ava giggled.

Jay never thought about why they both always went to school so early, and then the answer hit him. They simply wanted to spend time together. Jay smiled and kept his answer to himself.

It wasn't until the end of the day that they found out what Brendan thought about Jay making the team.

Jay and Ava were about to head out the doors to walk home when Brendan got Jay's attention. "Hey, loser," Brendan said and walked towards Jay. "I don't care if you're on the same team as me. You are not my friend. And we will never be friends. You better stay out of my way."

Brendan bumped shoulders with Jay as he passed him.

"What's your problem?" Jay said.

Brendan stopped and got in Jay's face. "You're my problem," Brendan shouted. "I wish you would go back to where you came from. Nobody wants you here."

"I want him here. And clearly your dad does…he picked him on his team, didn't he?" Ava said.

"Ava, stay out of this," Brendan said. "This is between me and the loser here. My dad may have picked him on the team, but what about his own dad…where's he? He probably doesn't even want to be around you," he said pointing right in Jay's face.

Jay couldn't believe Brendan said that. At that moment Jay felt anger that he never felt before. He clenched his fists and thought about hitting Brendan right then and there, but Ava must have sensed it, and grabbed Jay's arm. "You're such a jerk, Brendan. Jay let's go," Ava said and pulled Jay in the other direction. Jay resisted at first, but Ava pulled harder, and they went out the doors.

"Got you there, didn't I, loser? How does it feel to have a girl fight your battles," Brendan yelled after them.

Jay knew that Brendan and him wouldn't automatically be best friends now that they were on the same team. But he hoped that Brendan would stop picking on him at least. It was obvious that it was only going to get worse. At the beginning, he started to pick on Jay for the fun of it. Now he really didn't like Jay. He saw him as his competition—as his enemy. It didn't matter to him at all that they were teammates. This only meant he had more opportunities to make Jay's life miserable.

"I don't know if I even want to play hockey," Jay said as they walked across the field.

"Don't say that," Ava said softly.

"It's true. Why did I end up on his team? I never thought I would make A."

"That just means you're really good. You should be proud of yourself."

"I am. But I think I would rather play B. I wonder if I could drop down a tier."

"I don't think it really works that way."

"Maybe I don't have to play this year then. I could just go back to skating on my own."

"You're too good not to play hockey, Jay," Ava said. "And how bad can it get? I mean, you have to deal with it at school already. And you never know, maybe things will get better once you are teammates."

"I doubt it," Jay said. "But hopefully you're right."

"I'm always right," Ava said and smiled. "But either way, I'll always be here for you. We'll get through it together."

Jay couldn't imagine not having Ava as a friend. She was the person that had made the rest of last year bearable, and now she was his biggest fan, and in so many ways, his protector. She stood up to the mean Miss Wallace. She told Jay's mom the truth, and now she was standing up to Brendan. Without her, Jay imagined himself still sitting in that last bathroom stall every recess. Now he was an A hockey player, and he had a great friend. Like Ava said: *How bad could things get?*

The worst had to be over.

CHAPTER 27

At the rink, life was different. There were no teachers, principals, or many of the rules that may have protected Jay (even if those rules didn't actually work to protect Jay at his school). But in the dressing room, when the coaches weren't around, boys could be funny, cruel, and completely inappropriate. There were jokes in the locker room that you wouldn't tell at school. There were things you would do, that you wouldn't do at school. Boys would swear, fart as much as possible (even louder than Miss Wallace), tell dirty jokes, pick on teammates that they were friends with, and pick on teammates that they weren't friends with. Brendan was the one that took the lead in all of those areas. Jay saw what Brendan was like at school, and he knew he wasn't a good kid, yet everyone seemed to like him. At hockey, he was way worse, and people seemed to like him even more—that or maybe they were just afraid of him.

Jay could tell at the very first practice that Brendan thought he could do anything he wanted. Brendan didn't learn anything from the incident at tryouts. Instead, he treated it as another reason to get revenge on Jay.

When Jay pushed open the door to the dressing room, there were seven boys already there, including Brendan.

"Hey, loser, are you lost? This is the A dressing room, not the loser's dressing room," Brendan said.

Jay walked in and put his bag down at the spot closest to the door.

"You can't sit there," Brendan yelled.

"Leave me alone," Jay said, and he bent over and unzipped his bag

"Only if you move your stuff, loser."

"Where do you want me to move it?"

"Into the bathroom," Brendan replied.

"I'm not dressing in the bathroom," Jay said.

"You and your equipment are crap. You belong in the toilet."

Jay shook his head, and started to pull equipment out of his bag. He wasn't going to listen to Brendan.

"What are you doing. Move your crap!" Brendan yelled again.

Jay pulled out his shin pads, and put them behind him.

Brendan got up and walked over to Jay. "I said, move your crap," Brendan said and picked up Jay's open bag and threw it towards the bathroom. Several pieces of equipment flew out.

"Hey!" Jay shouted. He ran over to pick up the scattered pieces of equipment. As he grabbed his glove and elbow pad, he bent down to put them back in his bag, but Brendan shoved him from behind. Jay fell into his bag and scrambled to get up while some of his new teammates made fun of him and laughed.

Brendan laughed louder than them all. "What a loser," Brendan said, and he shoved Jay down again.

"Let him up already," another boy said. He was average height for their age, and was normally quiet, but he was built like a bulldozer. Jay didn't know who he was.

"Seriously, Mike? Are you sticking up for this piece of crap?" Brendan said.

"No," Mike replied.

"Better not be, or I'll make you dress in the bathroom, too," Brendan threatened.

Mike looked at Jay, and shook his head. Jay didn't know if Mike was shaking his head at Brendan, or if he was annoyed that he had to speak up for Jay.

Two other players pushed open the dressing room door, and Coach Brian walked in behind them.

With an adult now in the room, Jay was able to gather his stuff, and he headed back to the spot he sat at briefly before. When the coach left, Brendan said more nasty things to Jay, but Jay tuned him out.

Once Jay's skates hit the ice, he felt relieved. He did a few hard laps and felt like he was right where he was supposed to be. Jay simply wanted to play hockey, but he knew he had a lot to learn. Being out on the outdoor rink by himself, he never got the chance to shoot against a goalie, face defenders, pass or receive a pass from anyone else. Now that he was on an actual hockey team, he knew that he would make some mistakes. He was hoping the coaches and his teammates would be patient with him. Brendan, on the other hand, seemed to take advantage of any mistake Jay made.

The practice started with a few basic warm-up drills, and then the coach's had them work on their breakout. Jay struggled and messed up a few times. He didn't quite understand the different roles of the different positions. The coaches planned to make Jay a centerman, but they wanted to teach him the other positions as well. Jay was playing all the different roles on the breakout, and it became overwhelming.

The coach finally blew the whistle and the whole team gathered on one knee around the three coaches and the white board. Brendan's dad was trying to explain what Jay was supposed to do.

"Why is he even here," Brendan said interrupting his dad. "He's awful."

"Jay," Coach Steven said, "I need you to do a lap as hard as you can. Right now!"

Jay felt terrible. He felt bad that he messed up the drill, and now the coach was already punishing him in front of everyone. But Jay got up and did exactly what Coach Steven said. He took off as fast as he could from where he was, and skated as hard as he possibly could. He wanted to give it his all to make up for his mistake.

The coaches and the players all watched Jay skate the full length of the ice and return to where they all were.

"Whoa," several of the boys collectively said when Jay got back.

"*Whoa*, is right," Coach Steven said. "That's why he's here, Brendan."

Brendan tried to look unimpressed, but even though he would never admit it, he was amazed at what he saw—just like everyone else.

"Well? Anyone else wondering why Jay is here?" Coach Steven said.

"To show us all up?" a player named Kyle responded, and a few players snickered. Kyle Powell was the biggest and slowest person on the team.

"No, KP. To help us win," Coach Steven said. "Each one of you are here to do your best to help our team win. Each of you have certain skills that will help us do just that. From this day forward, I want you to look around, we are a team, gentleman. No one player is above the team. We will have to work together if we want to win this year. And of course, I want all of you to have fun. But winning is fun."

That's when Jay realized that he wasn't in trouble for messing up. Coach Steven was showing him off. Jay didn't feel as bad about messing up.

After that first practice, Jay had won some of his teammates over with his incredible skating ability. Some didn't care who was on the team, because like coach said, they wanted to win. Jay knew he was going to work his hardest and do his best to help them do that.

For the next several practices, Jay started to put all of his skills together. His passing improved, and he was comfortable on the breakout for both the right wing and centre positions. He had yet to learn other things like picking up his man on the backcheck, when to make a line change, and how to always stay in his position. He also didn't quite understand some of the rules like icing and offsides. But those were all skills and rules he would have to learn from playing games.

In the middle of October, he finally had his first game as a Saskatoon Renegade.

CHAPTER 28

Jay pulled his black, grey, and white Renegade Jersey over his head, then his shoulder pads, and shot his arms through the sleeves one at a time. He then stood up on his skates and tugged at the bottom of the sweater and rolled his shoulders to adjust it into place. He was thrilled that he was able to get a jersey with his favourite number three on the back. Now that he was almost fully dressed for his first game, he sat down and stared at the floor for a while, as he visualized being out on the ice.

Just like in the tryouts, Jay was a combination of nervous and excited. His mom, grandma, grandpa, and Uncle Dylan were all there watching. He wanted to play well for them. He wanted to play well for his team. He went over in his head all the things he had been learning the last few practices. He knew he had to stay on the boards in his end, and make sure if the puck came to him that he looked for the pass, or chip it out of the zone. He knew he had to cover his defenceman in his zone. He knew that he had to try to pick up the loose man on the backcheck. Those would be the hard things. Those were the things he had to remember. The skating, shooting, and hopefully scoring, would be easy.

Coach Steven, Coach Brian, and Coach Paul all entered the dressing room one by one. "The Zamboni is just finishing up," Coach Steven said. "I need everyone to listen up. These are the lines for tonight. Jackson left, Brendan centre, and Ryan right. You three will start upfront. Matt and Tommy you will start back on defense. Mike left, Kory centre, and Jay right. Your line is out second. Chase and Connor you'll be the next set of D. Justin left,

Tanner centre, Kyle right. Your line will be out third. Any questions?" He paused and looked around at each of them. "No? Alright, the Zamboni should be done out there, so you guys get out there, do your best tonight, and let's get the W."

With that, everyone jumped up, grabbed their stick, and headed out the door.

Jay did a few hard laps around their half of the ice, and as he skated, he glanced up in the stands to see where his family was sitting. He didn't want to look at them too often, but he was playing for them, and he always would. He wanted to make them proud.

Jay skated another hard lap around their zone, and then joined the rest of the team around the faceoff circle to stretch. As he stretched, he watched the other team. He tried to size them up, and tried to pick out their best players. Those would be the players he would compete against. Even though this was his first game, he was going to try to match their play, or be better than the best ones out there.

When Jay's team finished stretching and moved on to the horseshoe drill, Jay thought he was ready, but he wasn't. He missed his teammate with his first pass by two stick-lengths, and had to skate all the way down the ice to the other team's zone to get the puck back. Jay was embarrassed, and was hoping his family didn't see what happened. But he was too afraid to look up and see if they noticed.

Jay made it back into the lineup, and Brendan skated up behind Jay. "You shouldn't even be wearing that," Brendan said.

Jay thought something was wrong with his equipment. "Wearing what?" Jay asked.

"That jersey. You don't belong on this team. Go back to where you came from."

Brendan had been quiet the last few practices, and Jay thought things would be better with Brendan. Instead, Brendan waited to say something right before their first game. He wanted

Jay to fail. But it didn't work. Jay used Brendan's comments as fuel. *Skate harder, shoot harder, play harder,* Jay told himself.

"Thanks," Jay said.

Brendan gave Jay a confused look.

Jay's next turn at the horseshoe he made a perfect pass. He then skated hard, made the loop, caught the pass, skated in and snapped the puck through the goalie's five-hole. From that moment, Brendan gave Jay some fuel he needed, and now Jay was on fire.

Jay's very first goal came on his third shift. He received a pass on the boards in his team's zone, and he chipped the puck by the other team's defenceman. He raced to pick up the puck, and when he got it, he was on a breakaway. Nobody could catch him. He broke in on the goalie, swiftly deked to the left side, cut back to the right, and put the puck between the post and the goalie's skate. It was a beautiful goal. And he wasn't done yet.

Jay played that first game like he had been playing his entire life. He made some mistakes, but so does every hockey player. Either way, he gave it his all each shift he played. He skated hard on both ends of the ice, and never stopped moving. He brought an energy to the game that everyone noticed. His own team, the other team, people out there watching, all had the same thought when Jay was out there: *Who is this kid?*

Jay ended up scoring three goals, which his teammates said was a hat trick (he had never heard that before), and he picked up two assists. Their team ended up winning that game 7-2. Brendan had two goals, but no assists. Everyone knew that Jay was the best player that game. His teammates and coaches gave him compliments, patted him on the helmet, or shoulder pads. Coach Steven gave him the puck he scored his first goal with, and put a piece of white tape with the date written on it. Everyone in the dressing room was happy for him. Happy for how good their team was going to be that season. Everyone except Brendan.

CHAPTER 29

Jay was the star following that first game. But there were two people that he could not seem to win over: Brendan and Miss Wallace. The next day at school he had incidents with both of them.

The first incident happened in the morning when Jay asked to go to the washroom. He was making his way back to class when Miss Wallace stopped him in the hallway. He tried to get around her, but she moved in front of him, and looked at him right in his face. Jay was extremely uncomfortable.

"I heard you made the A hockey team," Miss Wallace said.

"I did," Jay replied. He started to think that maybe she was coming around, and was going to congratulate him. But he was wrong.

"I don't know how you fooled them," Miss Wallace said.

"Fooled who?" Jay was confused.

"Your coaches. I don't know why they would ever pick a brat like you. Let me guess, your mom phoned and complained so much that they put you on the team just to shut her up," Miss Wallace said harshly.

Jay looked at her in shock. Was he dreaming, or was she actually saying this to him? When Jay stood there stunned with a hurt look on his face, she smiled and walked past him.

Jay went back to class, and sat down in his desk. He didn't know how somebody could be so mean. He replayed the scenario in his mind with all the things he hoped would have happened. He wished while she was saying all this to him, the principal heard it all, and fired her on the spot. He wished that he could have told her that she was a mean, fat walrus, just to see her stunned and hurt for once. But most of all, he wished it would have not happened at all.

"Jay, what do you think?" Mr. Young asked, and Jay almost jumped out of his desk.

"Think about what?" Jay was too into wishing how the interaction with Miss Wallace could have gone differently, that he didn't hear what Mr. Young said.

"What a loser," Brendan said loud enough for the class to hear, and some kids snickered.

"If I'm a loser, and I have more goals and assists than you, then what does that make you?" Jay said back to Brendan.

"Come say that to my face," Brendan said and stood up from his desk.

"I think I just did."

"Brendan and Jay…to the hallway, right now!" Mr. Young said raising his voice.

Mr. Young had come to Jay's defense quite often when he saw Brendan picking on him, but this was the first time Jay tried to stand up for himself. The interaction with Miss Wallace right before this incident made Jay upset, and he wasn't going to let them bully him anymore. Jay got up and walked out of the classroom, while Mr. Young made sure there was distance between Jay and Brendan. Mr. Young closed the classroom door after them.

"Are we still doing this?" Mr. Young asked Brendan when they got into the hall. "Aren't you guys teammates? Can't you just find a way to work together?"

"I will never be teammates with him," Brendan replied.

"You know, I have coached a lot of hockey, and all the talent doesn't mean anything if you can't play on a team," Mr. Young said.

"I can play on a team…but not with him," Brendan said.

"And why not, Brendan? As far as I can see, there is nothing to hate Jay about. So, help me understand."

Brendan looked down at his feet and didn't say anything. "That's what I thought," Mr. Young continued. "If you can't come up with a good reason, then this ends now. This ends today. You are classmates. You are teammates. You don't have to like each other, but you can still work together. In other words, whatever this is between you two, it is officially done. You got it?"

As he was saying this, Miss Wallace was walking past them, and she glared at Jay, as if to say, *Like I said...brat.* Jay thought about how different Miss Wallace and Mr. Young were. They probably didn't like each other, but they were still able to work together.

"You got it?" Mr. Young said again to Brendan.

"Yeah," Brendan said.

"Now let's get back to class," Mr. Young said and opened the door and watched them both walk back to their desks.

"You okay," Ava whispered to Jay.

Jay nodded and smiled. But he didn't feel okay. The glare from Miss Wallace unnerved him.

About ten minutes later, there was a knock on the classroom door, and Mr. Young went over and opened it. Mrs. Clarke stood in the doorway, and her and Mr. Young spoke quietly for a moment. Then Mr. Young called Jay over and said Mrs. Clarke needed to speak to him.

Can this day get any worse, Jay wondered. *It's not even lunch time.*

Jay was in the hallway again, and this time Mrs. Clarke was the one closing the door. "I hear there was another situation with Brendan today," Mrs. Clarke said. "I was hoping you both grew out of this over the summer. Do you care to explain yourself?"

"Explain myself?" Jay asked.

"Yes, Miss Wallace told me that you were picking on Brendan this morning."

"What? It's the other way around," Jay said.

"Miss Wallace said you may say that. She seems to know all your tricks very well."

"I'm sorry, but I have to get back to class."

"I'm not done talking to you," Mrs. Clarke said.

"But I'm done talking to you," Jay said and he went to open the door, but she pulled it shut.

"I think we need to go to my office."

"I don't think so. I think I need to go home," Jay said and he started walking down the hallway. When Mrs. Clarke called after him, he started running, and pushed the door open to the back of the school. He wanted to get as far away as possible. This day felt like he was reliving a nightmare from the year before. Jay knew that he should not have run away from the principal like that, but he couldn't go through all those misunderstandings again.

At this point it was only about five minutes until lunch time, and he always went home for lunch, but he knew he was in trouble. When he got home, his grandparents wondered how he got home so fast, but before he could explain anything, a phone call came from his mom.

"Yes, he's here. He's fine. No there's nothing to worry about. You go back to class and we'll talk to him. It's fine. Everything is fine. We'll see you later," his grandma said in a calm voice into the phone. His mom was panicking on the other end.

When Jay's grandma hung up, she looked at him with concern. "That was your mom. She had to leave class because your principal called. She said you ran away from the school?"

Jay felt terrible. He knew this was a busy week for his mom. She had been studying for midterm exams, and she didn't need this kind of distraction.

His grandpa looked at him. "What's up, little buddy? What happened?"

"I ran away from the principal. I'm so sorry. I know it wasn't the right thing to do. But I got so frustrated. Miss Wallace said some awful things to me, and then Brendan was picking on me in class. I needed to get out of there."

"Good for you," Jay's grandpa said. "Something needs to be done at that school.

"John!" his grandma said.

"It's true, and you know it," his grandpa said.

"What kind of awful things did she say to you?" his grandma asked.

"It was bad. It was about my mom. I don't even want to repeat it."

"About your mom?" his grandma asked. "Jay, you need to tell us exactly what she said."

"She said she heard I made the A team, and she called me a brat, and said my mom probably phoned and complained so much that they put me on the team to shut her up."

Jay's grandma looked upset, and his grandpa looked like he was going to blow up.

"I'm marching to that school right now," Jay's grandpa said.

"John, sit down," Jay's grandma said calmy. "You are not going anywhere. We are going to sit down, eat some lunch, and figure out what to do."

Jay was relieved that his grandparents weren't upset at him. They directed all their anger towards the school. But he didn't know what was going to happen next. Was he going to be in trouble? Was he going to be suspended? And then the doorbell rang.

"That must be Ava," Jay said. "I totally forgot about her."

"Don't tell her that," Jay's grandpa said and chuckled.

Ava came home for lunch with Jay every day, but this time he accidentally left without her. Jay got up and went to answer the door, but Ava already let herself in. She was practically family and Jay's grandma and grandpa said she was welcome whenever.

"Oh, good, you are here," Ava said. She took off her shoes.

"Sorry, I didn't wait for you. Something happened," Jay said.

"Everyone knows something happened," Ava said. "It was

chaos at the school."

"Really?" Jay said. They both walked in to the kitchen and sat down at the table.

Jay's grandparents greeted Ava, and then she continued. "Really. Mrs. Clarke came to talk to Mr. Young again, and she was all stressed, then they both left the classroom, and then Mr. Young came back, and then left again. Everyone in our class was happy cause Math class got cut short, though. So, what happened?"

"The usual," Jay said, "Miss Wallace said some things, then there was that situation with Brendan, and I ran from Mrs. Clarke, and she called my mom."

"You ran from the principal?" Ava laughed. "Who runs from the principal?"

"I did. As fast as I could. I needed to get out of there. Maybe I won't go back...or maybe they won't let me back."

"They have to let you back! I need you there," Ava said, and she looked upset at the thought of Jay not going back.

Jay also couldn't imagine going to another school without her. Everything just spiraled out of control that morning.

During lunch they talked about the plan for the afternoon. Jay was going to miss the afternoon, and they would fill his mom in on what happened that night. They thought that his mom would probably want to set up a meeting at the school, and once again try and clear up all of these misunderstandings before things got out of hand like they did in grade six. But by the time lunch was almost over, Jay announced that he was going back to school that afternoon.

"Grandma and grandpa, I'm going to go back to school with Ava this afternoon. I'm going to go apologize to Mrs. Clarke for running away, because that wasn't right. I'm going to apologize to Mr. Young for any chaos I caused. And then I'll apologize to my mom tonight."

There was a lot of tension and anger when his grandparents talked about the school during that lunch hour. But that instantly all went away when Jay told them his plan.

"I think that's the best thing to do," his grandma said.

"I'm proud of you, little buddy," his grandpa added.

"Also," Jay said. "I don't think we should tell my mom about what Miss Wallace said about her. Not this week, anyway."

"I think that's another good idea," his grandma said.

Ava and Jay walked back to the school together. Halfway across the field, Ava reached out and held Jay's hand. Jay looked over and smiled at Ava. They walked hand in hand all the way to the back entrance of the school. They were a team.

That afternoon, Jay's plan worked. Mrs. Clarke was still upset, but with the help of Mr. Young, they explained everything that happened. Jay was ready to take responsibility for his mistakes, but he was also willing to stand up for himself. Stand up for what was right. Since he went back and took responsibility, there wasn't any suspension, or expulsion. Jay was welcomed back into Mr. Young's class.

When Jay got home from school, Jay's mom was already there. She was planning to stay late to study, but she was worried about Jay. She hugged him as soon as he got in the house.

"I was so worried about you, Jay-Jay," his mom said and hugged him tighter, and let him go. "Your principal called twice in the middle of my class and said you ran away and they didn't know where you went. I tried calling your phone, but it went straight to voicemail. I was so relieved when your grandma said you were okay."

"I'm sorry, mom," Jay said. "But everything is okay. It was all a big misunderstanding and I went back to school this afternoon."

"Are you going to tell me what happened?" his mom asked.

"It was nothing, I promise. I want you to focus on your studying."

Jay's mom raised her eyebrows and gave him a look. Jay

sounded like an adult. He smiled, and his mom didn't say anything else.

He was growing up.

CHAPTER 30

A few weeks later, at the beginning of November, Jay woke up one morning and something felt different. He felt something in his bones, and it wasn't growing pains. He shot up from his bed, and looked out the window. Jay smiled in delight. "It finally snowed!" he said to himself. Jay had been wishing for snow for months. Now, he couldn't wait for the outdoor rink to be flooded.

As the temperature continued to drop and more snow fell, each day, him and Ava would walk to school, and Jay would look over the boards and see if the rink was flooded and ready to go. It wasn't until almost two weeks later that Jay could tell it was thick enough to skate on. "I think I'm going to skip school today, go back home and get my skates, and spend the whole day on the rink," he said to Ava. "You good with walking the rest of the way to school?"

Ava laughed. "Are we supposed to all watch you from the classroom window? Mr. Young included?"

"That's a great idea. You can all cheer me on. Brendan, too."

Ava laughed again. "Let's get to school. You have plenty of time to go tonight," Ava said.

Tonight? Jay thought. He had never been out there with anyone else on the ice. But he was a hockey player now. He didn't have to feel embarrassed.

Jay and Ava walked the rest of the way to school, but that day was a blur. He could think about nothing else other than getting on that rink.

When he got home at the end of the day, he decided he

couldn't wait until morning. "Mom, would it be all right if I head to the rink after supper?" he asked.

Jay's grandma, grandpa, and mom all looked at each other briefly. They all had the same thought. Jay was finally comfortable enough to head out on the ice with all the other kids in the neighborhood. He was no longer afraid.

"Of course you can, Jay-Jay," his mom said.

Jay ate supper faster than he ever had. Not because he was so hungry, but because he wanted to get out on the rink. When he was done, Jay grabbed his stick, skates, gloves, and three pucks, and headed out towards the rink. After he opened the back gate, he could see a bunch of people already out there. From that distance, he could tell they were older kids by how fast they moved on the ice, and how loud the puck was when it hit the boards.

As he started out across the field, he counted seven or eight people out there. He got discouraged and thought about turning back. He enjoyed having the ice to himself, and he didn't know if these older kids would let him play. As he was thinking all of these things, he found that his legs kept walking toward the rink. He made it to the bench where he always laced up his skates, leaned his stick against the boards, and sat down. He looked over his shoulder and he could tell these were all high school kids that were much bigger than him. They were in the middle of a four against three hockey game, and were playing hard. There was a lot of yelling and an equal amount of laughter. Jay took a deep breath, unpacked his small bag, and started to put on his skates. When he was all ready, he stood up, walked to the opening, and waited until one of the teams stopped to dig the puck out of their net. *Here goes nothing*, he thought. Then he skated onto the ice, and bravely called out, "Can I play?"

All seven of them turned and looked him up and down. "Suit yourself, little man," the tallest one said. "But we aren't going to take it easy on you."

Jay smiled. The way he had been playing that season so far, he felt like he could have stepped on the ice with anyone.

"Okay, kid, you'll be on their team," another older player said and pointed with his stick to the other side of the ice. It was the team that had the three players. With Jay, it would now be an even game of four against four.

Jay skated over to the older kids on the other side of the rink. "What's up, Jay," one older boy said as he stood leaning his chin on the top of his hockey stick. "Nice skates."

"Oh, hey, Tyler!" Jay said. It was Ava's older brother, and Jay was wearing Tyler's old skates. Tyler was fifteen, and a great hockey player. Jay was happy to see a familiar face.

The game started without a face off. The other team had possession of the puck before the guys took a break and Jay showed up. Once the game started, Jay could tell that even though he was the youngest of the group, these older kids were a variety of different levels. Some looked like A hockey players, like Tyler, and others couldn't skate that well.

At the beginning, no one passed the puck to Jay—not even Tyler. All of the older boys were bigger and stronger, and just like they said, they didn't take it easy on him. But this only pushed Jay to try as hard as he could. The other players were out there to have fun, but Jay was out there to challenge himself and get better. After a while, Jay's teammates saw that he could play, and they passed him the puck.

Some of the older boys on the other team also started to get frustrated. Jay stole the puck from one of them in the corner, and the kid shouted, "Get away from me you little gnat," and slashed Jay in the leg.

Jay went down and he felt a burning in his shinbone. He thought about what happened at the first recess game the year before, and wondered if he had just made another enemy. But Tyler saw what happened, skated over as fast as he could, and got in the other boy's face. Tyler threatened to pound the other boy into the ice if he ever did that again, and another teammate helped Jay up. Nothing like that happened again that night.

When the game finished, the older boys said that Jay could come out and play with them any time. The boy that slashed him even apologized and said that next time Jay could be on his team instead.

Befriending older kids like that, and having them stick up for him, felt good for a change. He knew that if someone like Brendan was out there giving him a hard time, one of his new friends might even threaten to "pound him into the ice" as well. It was also pretty cool that Jay was able to skate with Tyler. If he had a great hockey player to look up to, and play with on the outdoor rink, Jay knew that he could learn a lot from him and become even better. It was the first time in a while that Jay felt like he fit in somewhere, and it felt good to know he could head out on the outdoor rink whenever he wanted. And already the next day, he would start his morning practices.

CHAPTER 31

Jay was happy to have his morning practices back. As much as he enjoyed playing with Tyler and the older boys at night, there was nothing that could replace being on the rink in the morning. To Jay, it was the absolute best way to start his day.

His mom and grandparents thought he would give up when the early mornings caught up to him. They thought there was no way he would be able to do it every day and thought he would tire himself out. But he never did. Not only did he still go out every morning—even on days he had a practice or a game—he also went out to play with Tyler and the older boys whenever he could.

With all the hockey that he was playing, Jay's hockey skills started to reach the next level. Jay was still the best skater that many people had seen, but he was also becoming a well-rounded hockey player. Jay was such a quick learner, but once he started to put everything together, he showed that he had a natural instinct for the game. He could read where the puck would end up, where he should be, and he always appeared to be in the right spot. Others would say that the puck followed him out there. It was remarkable that this was a kid that recently started playing hockey and hadn't watched much of it either.

In no time at all, when Jay would play with Ava's brother Tyler, and the other bigger boys, Jay started to stand out amongst them as well. Even the kids that were first annoyed by Jay, started to become in awe of him. Many wanted to be out there on the ice with him simply to see what he would do next.

"My brother says that you are better than most kids on his

team," Ava said one day when they made the short walk home from school.

"I don't know about that," Jay said. He felt the heat rise in his face.

"Seriously. He told my parents that he thinks you are going to make the NHL."

"If anyone is going to make it, it's your brother," Jay said.

Tyler was the captain of the U18 Renegade team, but he should have been playing city-wide AA or even playing on the Contacts or Blazers. He got cut because he was "too young" and "too small", but he was proving everyone wrong.

"Maybe you'll both make it," Ava said as they reached the back gate to her yard.

Jay never thought about a future in hockey. He honestly never thought that far ahead. All he wanted to do was skate and play hockey every day, so the more he thought about it, making the NHL seemed like a great idea.

"Want to come over for bit?" Ava asked.

"I have a game tonight, so I should go home, eat, and get ready."

"Maybe I can come watch you...I don't think Tyler has a game tonight, so maybe my parents will come, too."

"Sounds good to me. I'll text you after supper," Jay said, and he closed the gate. Jay walked back to his grandparent's house hoping Ava could come watch. He wanted his best friend there.

Jay texted Ava when he finished supper to find out if Ava and her parents were going to come watch, and they were. Jay found out that Tyler was also going to come watch. It would be the first time that Jay had any fans outside of his mom, grandparents, and his uncle. It meant a lot to Jay to know that he had them in his corner.

On the ride to the hockey rink, Jay knew he was going to play his heart out.

CHAPTER 32

During warmup, Jay was skating hard around his team's half of the rink. As he stopped striding, he glided for half a lap, and Brendan skated up beside him. "Did you see Ava and her family came to watch me play?" Brendan said. "I'm going to score Ava a hat trick tonight."

"They didn't come to watch you play," Jay said, and his fist tightened around his hockey stick.

"They sure did. Ava is my girlfriend," Brendan said.

Rage surged through Jay's veins, and he instantly wanted to crosscheck Brendan in the facemask. Jay didn't know why this bothered him so much. He knew that Ava didn't like Brendan, but hearing him say that, almost sent Jay over the edge. Jay restrained himself and skated away. He could hear Brendan's annoying laugh from behind him. Jay was thrilled to have fans come to watch him play, but Brendan, like always, had to do something to ruin it.

Brendan's not going to score Ava a hat trick, I'm going to score Ava a hat trick, Jay thought as he skated over to stretch with the rest of team. He hated the fact that he had to watch Brendan in the middle of the circle leading the team in stretches. Jay didn't think Brendan was a good leader at all.

To make things worse, a few games ago, Coach Steven also put Jay on the same line as Brendan. Coach was secretly hoping that being linemates may bring the two boys together. His son was the problem, but he knew that if they could become real teammates, that line would be unstoppable.

So far, both players played amazing on the same line, but they didn't play together. Brendan refused to pass Jay the puck, and missed out on so many goal-scoring opportunities. Jay on the other hand, set Brendan up many times, and collected a pile of assists.

Jay knew that with Ava in the stands, the chances of Brendan passing him the puck were slim. And it would be hard for Jay to pass the puck to Brendan so he could score Ava a hat trick. *Why do we have to be on the same line? Why tonight?* Jay wondered as they lined up for the faceoff against the Martensville Marauders.

On their first shift, it was clear that Brendan wasn't going to pass Jay the puck. On a rush over the red line, their left winger, Mike, slid the puck up to Brendan, but there were two defensemen back. Jay rushed ahead in order to find some open ice. Brendan toe-dragged the puck and put it through the defenseman's skates, and then blew past him. Jay was wide open as the other defensemen went to decrease the gap between him and Brendan. Jay called out and waited with his stick on the ice hoping Brendan would pass it over. Instead, Brendan picked up speed, went wide around the defensemen, and cut in hard on the net. As the goalie slid across, Brendan put it top-shelf over the goalie's shoulder. It was a great goal, with a lot of effort. Brendan could have simply passed the puck over to Jay, and they would have had a much easier chance to score. But it was hard to argue against such a nice goal.

"That's one," Brendan said as Jay and the rest of the team went over to congratulate him.

Jay tried to pat Brendan on the shoulder—like the rest of the teammates did that were on the ice—but Brendan moved out of the way. "Don't touch me," Brendan growled.

Jay pulled back his hand and was left there feeling awkward. Was he not supposed to go over to congratulate Brendan any time he scored? Wouldn't that look like he was being a bad teammate?

The next time Jay's line was on the ice, Brendan scored

another goal. This time their defensemen, Tommy, shot a puck on net, and Brendan got the rebound and tapped it in. Jay didn't go over to Brendan this time. He skated right to the bench.

"That's two," Brendan said to Jay back at the bench. "Ava's going to be so happy when I tell her I scored all these goals for her."

"Shut up, Brendan," Jay said quietly.

"You shut up, loser. Not my fault you can't score."

Jay made up his mind that he was going to do whatever it took to score a goal the next time out. Jay was about to play angry—not angry at the other team—angry at his centerman. Jay thought that if he could score more goals than Brendan, that would shut Brendan up once and for all.

The next time Jay was out, the puck was on the left side of the ice in the neutral zone. Mike and Brendan were battling against the boards, and Jay left his position and hustled over to help. He was able to pick up a loose puck, and he skated hard into the Martensville zone. When he got to the top of the circle, he switched gears and went around the defenseman. He cut to his forehand, and fired a hard wrist shot on the goalie's short side between his pad and blocker. The puck hit the inside of the post and went in. Jay raised his arms and his linemates came and congratulated him. Meanwhile, Brendan skated to the bench.

"Jay, nice wheels out there, and nice goal," Coach Steven said when Jay got back to the bench. "But you were on the wrong side of the ice. You need to play your position."

Jay knew he wasn't playing his position when he went over there. But he did that to show Brendan what he could do, and hopefully shut him up. It didn't work.

"Nice one, loser. Glad you're too dumb to stay on your own side of the ice," Brendan said.

It felt like Jay couldn't win. No matter what he did, Brendan would make some sort of comment. Jay had to do what Ava always told him to do: ignore him. Jay looked up to where Ava was siting, and she was smiling. Jay wondered if it was because of his goal. He imagined it was, and that made him feel a bit better.

They finished the period and Jay's team was up 3-1. The entire period, Brendan never passed it to Jay once. Jay had a few nice passes to Brendan, but Brendan wasn't able to score. The other team started to shut their line down, because they weren't able to work together.

Luckily, Mike, their left winger, would pass to either of them. He was the only one that wasn't playing with a grudge out there. In the second period, he had the puck behind the other team's net, and he plowed his way to the other side, and saw Jay open in the slot. He passed it to Jay, and just as he was about to shoot it, Brendan took the puck off his stick, shot it, and hit the post on a wide-open net.

The other team broke out of their zone, and Jay had to hustle back, and help stop an excellent scoring chance. Brendan didn't even bother backchecking.

"Thanks for getting in my way, loser," Brendan said back on the bench. "I could have had my hat trick."

"You're the one that took the puck off of my stick and hit the post on a wide-open net. That was embarrassing," Jay shot back.

"Yeah, what was that all about, Brendan?" Coach Steven came over and asked. "Taking the puck from teammates now?"

"I didn't know it was him. I thought it was the defenseman," Brendan tried to argue.

"Maybe you should play with your head up then. Know what's going on around you," Coach Steven said.

Jay didn't say anything, but smiled at Brendan as he was getting called out by his dad.

"Shut up, loser," Brendan said under his breath.

"Did you just tell me to shut up?" Coach Steven asked his son.

"No, I was talking to, Noble," Brendan replied.

"Jay didn't say anything," Coach Steven said. "You know what, I'm tired of this. You're going to miss your next shift. And if you can't get along with your linemates by the next time around, you're going to miss another shift."

"That's not fair," Brendan complained.

"Enough already. What you're doing isn't fair," Coach Steven said. By now everyone on the bench was watching and listening. "You have the C on your jersey. Now act like a captain, or I'll find someone else that deserves it more."

Brendan sat back on the bench, while Tanner—another centreman—jumped up to Jay's line. The Renegades now had two centerman that were going to double shift until Brendan was ready to rejoin the game.

On their first shift together, after breaking out of their zone, Tanner took the puck through the neutral ice, and went wide. Jay picked up speed to the open ice. It was a two-on-one and Tanner slid the puck over to Jay, and he sped towards the net. The goalie went down, and as he did, Jay shot the puck in the top right corner of the net for his second goal. His linemates came over and patted him on the helmet and shoulder pads, and said, "nice goal."

"Nice pass,' Jay said to Tanner. It felt good to be on a normal line once again.

After that goal, Coach Steven put Brendan on a different line, and Tanner became Jay's new linemate. With no more distractions, Jay played awesome hockey for the rest of the game. Jay was often the first one in their zone, and the first one backchecking. He battled in the corners, and was able to come up with the puck more often than not. He took control of the game each time he was out there, and he could have had many goals, but he set up Mike and Tanner twice each, instead. Jay finished the game with two goals, and four assists. Brendan managed to get one more goal that game to get his hat trick, and the Renegades won 9-3.

As they were skating off the ice, Brendan cut in front of Jay.

"I can't wait to tell Ava I got her a hat trick," Brendan said looking over his shoulder.

"Whatever, I got more points than you," Jay said.

They both made it to the gate, and stepped off the ice, and started walking towards the dressing room.

"A hat trick is way better than any assists, loser," Brendan said.

"What are you talking about, son," Coach Steven said overhearing their argument. "I would take six points over three, any day of the week...great game, Jay."

Coach Steven stepped between them to unlock the dressing room door.

Brendan didn't say anything else.

When Jay got out of the dressing room, he wanted to go find Ava, but before he could get very far, someone grabbed Jay by the shoulder. Jay turned around and it was Mike's grandpa. "Jay, you had a heck of a game out there today," Mike's grandpa said.

"Thanks," Jay said. He had never talked to Mike's grandpa before, but he knew who he was.

"But, let me tell you a secret," Mike's grandpa added and he looked very serious. "You are the fastest skater out there. One of the fastest I have seen at your age. You should beat everybody to the puck. Every time. Never let the other team get there before you do. Remember, never stop skating."

"I won't," Jay said.

Mike's grandpa nodded and patted Jay on the shoulder. "Heck of player. Heck of a game."

Jay continued on his way to go look for Ava. *That was intense,* Jay thought. Mike's grandpa wasn't just an ordinary fan. Mike's grandpa used to play in the NHL. Mike's grandpa knew what he was talking about. Jay walked away feeling taller.

Jay walked over to Ava and her family. They were all smiling.

"Great game, Jay!" Ava said.

"Yeah, great game," her mom and dad added.

"Man, you're fast. Must be my old skates," Tyler said.

As he talked to Ava and her family, Jay saw Brendan walk by with his dad, and they were arguing. Nobody said a word to them at all, and Brendan thankfully didn't stop to say that he scored Ava a hat trick.

"I wonder what that's all about," Ava's dad said.

"They're probably arguing about me," Jay said.

"Was Brendan being a jerk to you again?" Ava asked.

"Something like that," Jay replied. He didn't want to think about Brendan. He wanted to enjoy the good parts of the game.

"Is that why he was taken off your line?" Tyler asked.

"Pretty much," Jay said.

"Man, if you two could only get along, you two would put up so many points each game," Tyler said.

"That's exactly what coach said," Jay told Tyler.

"Instead, he refuses to pass you the puck," Tyler added.

"And takes the puck right off my stick," Jay said.

"I saw that! That was terrible," Ava said. "Oh, well. You played amazing. Way better than he did."

"Thanks, Ava," Jay said.

Eventually, Jay's grandpa, grandma, and mom made their way over to Jay. "Hey, we were waiting for you at the front," Jay's mom said to Jay as she ruffled his hair. She then looked down at her hand, and instantly regretted touching his wet, sweaty hair.

Several other parents came over, patted Jay on the shoulder, and said, "Great game."

"Your talented son was too busy talking to his fans," Ava's mom said.

"If he keeps playing the way he did, we'll have to wait for him a lot longer after the crowds disperse," Jay's grandpa said.

"Soon he'll have to start signing autographs," Ava added to the fun.

Jay stood there as they talked about him. He wasn't used to getting so much praise from everyone. It was almost all of last year that he heard so much of the opposite each day.

He readjusted his hockey bag on his shoulder.

"Well, kiddo, should we head home?" his mom asked.

"We'll head out, too," Ava's mom said.

They all walked out together. As they made their way out of the rink, Jay received more congratulations along the way.

"You're quite the star, kiddo," his mom said.

That night at the rink, Jay had a lot of positive attention on him, and with the way he was playing, he would have to get used to it.

CHAPTER 33

About halfway through the season, Jay made the full-time transition to playing centre. He was just too fast to be stuck on the wing. As a result, he no longer had to worry about being on the wrong side of the ice, and he didn't have to be on the same line as Brendan. And since they were both centremen, they were rarely on the ice together. Brendan still picked on Jay in the dressing room, and at school, but there were so many things that were going well for Jay. Since people were giving him praise for many things, it was easier to ignore whatever Brendan was trying to do to him.

Jay's team was 11-5 on the season up to that point, but they easily could have been undefeated. Between Jay and Brendan, they had so much talent, and both could almost score on command. But the whole team wasn't getting along, due to Brendan's leadership as captain, and his constant attempts to make Jay's life miserable. Finally, before one game, something happened and everything changed.

In the dressing room at Agri Twins arena, before a game against the Saskatoon Flyers, Jay unzipped his hockey bag.

"Hey, loser, you should just go home tonight. We don't need you," Brendan said.

Jay was coming into that game leading the team in points with an impressive 17 goals and 20 assists in 16 games. Brendan had 23 goals but only 5 assists at that point.

"Can you quit calling me a loser already," Jay said. "I have more points than you. Which means you're the loser. Or are you too stupid to figure that out?"

It was almost the same thing that Jay said to Brendan in class earlier in the season. But this time, Jay didn't have Mr. Young to protect him.

Brendan's face turned red and then he snapped. He had been benched a few times already from his dad for picking on Jay, but at this point, he didn't care. He was going to make Jay pay. Without saying anything else, Brendan got up, raced towards Jay, and grabbed his hockey bag. Jay got up and tried to grab it back, but Brendan yanked it away, ran over to the showers, dumped all of the equipment in there, and threw the bag.

"Don't do it," Jay said as he fought his way over there.

But it was too late. Brendan turned all three shower heads on, and the water poured onto Jay's equipment. Brendan walked out of the showers howling with laughter as he let Jay by.

Jay scrambled to turn the water off in the hopes of saving some of his equipment, but he also got soaked in the process. When he got the water off, he picked up a soaking wet glove, and threw it at his water-filled hockey bag. He left his equipment, walked out of the showers, and slumped down to the floor. There was no rage. No sadness. He felt numb.

The rest of the players were in shock. Brendan was the only one with a smile on his face.

"What is happening in here?" Coach Steven came barging in, followed by Mike, who went out to get the coach. Coach Steven looked at Jay sitting on the ground, soaking wet. "Jay, you alright?"

Jay couldn't speak. He simply shook his head.

"Somebody please tell me what is going on," Coach Steven said. He went over to the showers, and looked in. Then he looked at his son, and Brendan's smile faded. "Brendan, was this you?"

"The loser deserved it," Brendan said.

"Are you kidding me right now?" Coach Steven said. "Look at what you did to his equipment. Jay can't play tonight. And for what? Because you're jealous?"

"I'm not jealous of him. He sucks," Brendan said.

"He sucks? He works harder than anyone else on this team. He has more points than anyone else in the league. What sucks is your attitude," Coach Steven said. He walked over to his son, reached behind him, and grabbed his jersey off the hook. "You won't be needing this tonight, either. And this C on here, you don't deserve that anymore."

The dressing room was normally a lively place, but no one moved or made a sound.

"Everyone get dressed. We have a game to play tonight. Except for you, Brendan," Coach Steven said to break the silence. Coach Steven walked over to Jay and crouched down. "I'm sorry, Jay. I'll get this cleaned up for you."

Coach Steven went into the shower and did his best to wring out Jay's hockey bag and some of the equipment. Jay made his way to the spot he was sitting at before, and looked off into space as everyone got ready. He didn't know what to do. He didn't know what to think. He felt defeated.

Once his team went out on the ice, Jay texted his uncle Dylan, and told him that he needed him in the dressing room.

"What's up, Neph?" Uncle Dylan said when he entered the dressing room. He took one look at Jay and stopped. "What happened? Why aren't you dressed? Why are you all wet?"

Uncle Dylan was struggling to put it all together.

"Brendan," Jay said.

Uncle Dylan's face flushed with rage. "I'll be right back."

"Unc, stop," Jay said calmly. "Don't."

Jay knew his uncle was going to go find Brendan and do something or say something he shouldn't.

His uncle stopped, took a deep breath, and regained his composure. "Let's get you home."

Uncle Dylan took off his big winter jacket, and wrapped it around Jay. "This won't be a fun walk to the parking lot, but hopefully this will keep you from instantly turning into a human-sized ice cube."

Then, Uncle Dylan went over to Jay's hockey bag, and lifted it onto his shoulder. "This is ridiculous. Absolutely ridiculous."

Despite his best efforts, Coach Steven wasn't able to magically dry all of Jay's equipment, and the entire bag was sopping wet.

"I can carry it," Jay said.

"No, I got this," his uncle said.

Before they left the dressing room, Uncle Dylan called Jay's grandpa and told him to meet them at his vehicle.

Jay walked out of that rink with his uncle, and he stared at the ground the whole way. Thoughts of quitting the team swam around in his head.

When his grandpa saw Jay walking through the parking lot, he didn't need to ask what happened. Part of him didn't even want to know the details. "You'll be all right, little buddy," his grandpa said, and he opened the door for his grandson.

Jay, his uncle, and his grandpa were mostly silent on the short drive from the arena. They just wanted to get home.

Back at the house, Uncle Dylan took Jay's equipment and hung everything up on a drying rack in the basement bathtub. He doubted it would even be dry in time for Jay's practice the following day.

After a hot shower to warm up, Jay met his uncle, grandpa, and grandma in the living room.

"Feeling better?" his grandpa asked.

Jay plopped down on the couch. "Not really. I think I'm done. I don't want to play anymore."

It hurt Jay's family to see him like that.

"What happened to you was brutal," Uncle Dylan said. "And I know it doesn't seem like it, but if you keep going, that shows everyone that nothing can stop you. And honestly, Neph, that quality alone will take you far in life. I mean, just look at your mom."

His uncle had a point. His mom was a great example of someone who always worked hard and never gave up on her dreams.

"Your uncle is right," his grandpa said. "It's so frustrating that this is happening, but things will getter better."

"It will always work out, it always does," his grandma added.

"I don't know if you'll be able to practice tomorrow, but your equipment will be dry for the weekend, and I think you should go out to Regina, and show them all, that you'll never quit," Uncle Dylan said.

Suddenly Jay remembered the hockey books he read. All the hockey greats had one thing in common: they all overcame obstacles and never gave up. This was just one missed game, and it wasn't going to stop him.

As for the Renegades, there wasn't any coming back from what happened before the game that night. They were missing their two best players, and everyone was off their game. They lost 5-0 against a team they beat twice already that season. What Brendan did, had an impact on everyone.

Later that night, Jay and his uncle went to the garage to shoot some pucks. They were playing a game to see who could hit the corners of the net the most, when Jay's mom pulled up on the driveway.

She got out of her black SUV and rushed over to the open garage holding her phone. "Are you okay, Jay-Jay?"

"Yeah, I'm fine," Jay said.

"Are you sure? I got this strange text from Coach Steven." She held out her phone so Jay could read it.

I hope Jay is doing alright. Can you tell him that he is the new captain of the Renegades?

"Hey, Unc, you won't believe this…they made me captain."

"I believe it," Uncle Dylan said. "No one deserves it more than you."

Jay's mom squinted her eyes. "If Brendan is no longer captain. That means Coach Steven took it away from him. What did Brendan do to you, Jay-Jay?"

"Let's just say that Brendan really wanted to clean Jay's equipment, so he gave it a shower," Uncle Dylan said. "But the problem is he did it before the game and not after, so it didn't have time to dry."

"Jay, what in the world is your crazy uncle talking about?" Jay's mom asked.

Jay laughed. "That's basically what happened, mom. I'll tell you the whole story inside. But first—" Jay turned back to the net and released a laser of a wrist shot to the top right corner.

"Whoa," his mom said.

Jay looked over at his uncle. "I win."

Uncle Dylan grinned. "You sure did, Captain."

CHAPTER 34

Jay didn't get a chance to see the "C" on his jersey until his first overnight hockey tournament in Regina, Saskatchewan. He pulled his jersey over his head, over his shoulder pads, and stretched it down over the waist of his hockey pants. He looked down at the "C" newly sewn on to his jersey and ran his fingers over it—almost as if to see if it was actually real. It felt good to be captain. A few short months ago, Jay would have never imagined in a million years that he would be the captain of a hockey team.

Jay could feel Brendan's eyes on him as he put on his jersey, but he did his best to ignore him. Jay wasn't going to let Brendan ruin this for him.

"Alright, the ice is almost ready…helmets on," Coach Steven said as he leaned on the door to look out at the rink. "Let's go out there, work hard on both ends of the ice, move the puck around, and get us another W. You boys ready?"

"YEAH!" everyone hollered—except Brendan.

Chad, their goalie, stood up and waddled his way to the dressing room door. The rest of the team followed.

Earlier that day, Jay got to miss the afternoon of school, so that him, his mom, grandma, and grandpa could all pack up and drive down to Regina. Jay felt tired after the two-hour drive, checking in at the hotel, and eating supper at a restaurant, but as he stepped out of the dressing room right behind their goalie, he felt energized.

As he looped around their half of the ice, he felt different. Having the "C" on his jersey gave him a confidence he never had before. It wasn't just about playing the game and doing his best, it was about motivating his teammates, and leading by example. Others would see him as being the best player on the Saskatoon Renegades—it was labeled right there on his jersey.

In that first game as captain, Jay led the Renegades to a 6-3 win against a tough Regina Blues team. He had two goals and two assists in the win. Jay was the official leader on the ice, but back at the hotel, not everyone respected his new role.

Jay didn't spend a lot of time with the other boys in his class, or on his team, and didn't know what they were up to. He started to realize that some of the kids were getting into trouble. Kyle bragged about plugging a toilet with paper towel in the hotel lobby before the game. Brendan thought it was hilarious. Jay thought it was stupid.

On these tournaments Jay also found out—almost the hard way—that they liked to play nasty pranks on each other. It was almost like the hockey part of the tournament didn't matter. As a leader, Jay would have to change that.

When they got back to the hotel after the game, Jay and his mom were in their room, when there was a knock on the door. Jay went over, looked through the peephole, and saw that it was Ryan and Tommy. Jay opened the door.

"Hey, Captain, come hang with us," Ryan said.

Jay was hesitant to go. Ryan was best friends with Brendan, and he wondered if it was a trap.

"I don't know. We have an early game tomorrow, and Coach said we had to be in our rooms by ten," Jay said. "What are you guys up to?"

"We're going to relax and watch a movie, and we need our captain there," Tommy said.

Jay looked back at his mom, and he didn't even have to say anything. "Go, have fun," she said.

Jay put his shoes on and followed Ryan and Tommy to a room down the hall. Ryan knocked and Jackson opened the door.

Jackson was a tall and gangly kid with light red hair. He was the type of kid that was smoother at skating than he was at walking. When he opened the door, he was eating a powdered donut, and he turned and yelled into the room with his mouth full, "Captun's hur!"

Jay grimaced when he saw a puff of powdered sugar and pieces of chewed up donut fly out Jackson's mouth.

Ryan held the door open for Jay, and he walked into the room. The room was identical to the one he was staying in, and he saw that there were four other players on the team already in there—including Brendan.

Tanner was sitting on the bed closest to the door, with his back against the headboard. After scarfing down the rest of his donut, Jackson sat beside him. Brendan and Kyle were siting on the bed near the window, and they both had their hoods on and were wearing sunglasses. Jay thought they looked ridiculous, but they were probably trying to look cool. Jay noticed that Brendan held what looked like a pen to his mouth, and then blew out a white vapour. Then he passed it over to Kyle, and the smell of cotton candy filled the room. Jay felt uncomfortable.

"Noble, you want some?" Kyle said holding out the pen.

"No, I'm good," Jay said. He didn't want to mess around with what they were doing.

"Come on Captain, stop being such a loser," Brendan said, and reached out and grabbed the pen back from Kyle. He held it out to Jay. "Just try it."

"That's not my thing," Jay said. He knew it was a bad idea, and immediately thought about leaving. He stood there awkwardly.

"If he doesn't want it then he doesn't want it," Tommy interrupted. "You guys are idiots for vaping, anyway. But can we start the movie?" Tommy said.

"Hit play!" Tanner shouted and opened a bag of ketchup chips.

Jackson opened a bag of Cheezies, and all the attention shifted towards the variety of snacks. "Captain, there's a chair by the desk you can sit in," Jackson said.

Jay went over and sat in it. The boys passed around a couple bags of chips, and each of them grabbed handfuls.

As everyone settled in, Jay still felt left out. It seemed like all of them were friends already, and he had never hung out with them before. He felt like he didn't belong. He suddenly wondered what other players like his linemate Mike were up to.

A box of Tim Hortons donuts was also passed around, and it made its way to Brendan.

"Noble, you want a donut?" Brendan asked.

Jay recognized that Brendan called him something other than "loser" for the first time in forever. He thought that was strange. "No, I'm good," Jay replied.

"*No, I'm good. No, I'm good,*" Brendan said mimicking Jay. "Can you say anything else? But come on, man. You won't vape with us, but you can at least have the last donut."

"Fine," Jay said. *What's the worst thing that could happen from eating a donut?* Jay thought.

Brendan held the box open, and Jay reached in and grabbed the Boston cream donut—it was one of his favourites. Brendan tossed the box on the floor, and Jay sat back down.

"Jay, stop!" Ryan shouted just as Jay was about to take a bite. "Don't eat that!"

Jay looked around and saw everyone was looking at him in a weird way—almost like they were all waiting for him to take a bite. "What did you do to it?" Jay said. He wondered if they dropped it on the floor or something. He examined the donut closely, and saw that the hole where they fill the donut with cream, looked bigger than normal. It looked like someone stuffed something inside.

"Ah, common, Fitz," Brendan said. "Why didn't you let the loser eat it?"

"Because I want to win tomorrow. We don't need our captain crapping his pants all day," Ryan said to Brendan. Then he turned to Jay. "They put chocolate laxative in it as a prank, so don't eat it."

"You guys are idiots," Jay said about to throw the laxative filled donut in the garbage. He knew he should have never trusted them.

"Hey, give that to me," Brendan said. "We can still use it on someone else."

Jay held on to it and looked at Brendan. "You're not going to do this to anybody on my team."

"Your team? Look around, this is my team. You're only here so we could prank you. Nobody likes you, loser," Brendan said.

"Loser? You're the real loser, and everyone knows it," Jay said. "Even your own dad took the C away from you, and gave it to me."

"That's it, you're dead!" Brendan said bolting out of the bed towards Jay.

Jay had nowhere to go, and he put his arms up in defense. As soon as Brendan got close enough, he took a swing at Jay. Using the move that his uncle Dylan showed him, Jay knocked Brendan's swinging right hand away with his left, and with his right hand he shoved the donut into Brendan's mouth, and smooshed it all over his face.

Brendan wiped his face and was spitting the laxative filled donut all over the floor. Some of the other boys froze not believing what just happened, and others thought it was awesome and started laughing. Ryan and Jackson jumped up and got in between the two.

"Let them go at it," Kyle said.

"No, we can't let our two best players kill each other," Ryan said.

Jay pushed his way to the door.

"You're dead, loser. You are so dead," Brendan said, and he

kept spitting on the floor. "You better watch your back."

"Let's get out of here before he craps his pants," Jackson said.

"See'ya later, crappy!" Tanner called out, and everyone but Brendan laughed.

Jay's teammates were leaving with him, but he was worried about what Brendan would do to him, and when he would do it.

Jay and the rest of the guys—except Kyle—left the room laughing.

"Where to now?" Ryan asked.

Before anyone could reply, their coach appeared.

"Hey, fellas," Coach Steven said walking towards them. "You need to quiet down out in the hallways."

"Sorry, Coach," they all said in unison.

"Is Brendan in our room?"

"Yeah, he's in there. Watch out for the donut he spit all over the place," Ryan said.

"What?" Coach said, confused.

Ryan told their coach what happened, and as he finished, Brendan and Kyle came out.

"Dad, Jay smashed a donut in my face, and made a mess of our room. Some captain he is, huh?" Brendan said.

"You know what, Brendan. It sounds like you got a taste of your own medicine...I'm not sure you should be this far away from the toilet, son," Coach Steven said.

All of Jay's teammates exploded with laugher. Coach Steven did not believe his son at all. The way he saw it, his boy got a little bit of what he deserved, and hopefully he would eventually learn his lesson.

"Alright, alright, quiet down," Coach Steven said. "I want you guys all in your own rooms by ten. We have two games tomorrow, and I want you all to be rested. That clear?"

"Yes, Coach," they all said in unison again.

"Now get out of here...I need to go talk to my son."

Jay and Ryan started walking down the hallway, and the rest of the guys followed.

"Brendan's going to kill you for what you did back there, you know that, right?" Ryan said to Jay.

"I know. But he had it coming. I just wish he would stop. We don't have to be friends, but our team would be so much better if we could be civil."

"Civil?" Ryan asked.

"Yeah, civil. If we could just get along," Jay said. "Isn't Brendan your best friend?"

"Yeah," Ryan said. "But he's being stupid lately. He's taking things too far. I'm sorry for what we did to you at school last year. You're a good guy, Noble. And our best player."

"Thanks, Fitz," Jay said. Ryan saying all of that meant a lot to him. If he could win Ryan over, maybe he could win others over, too.

"Where to captain," Jackson said from behind them.

Jay stopped and turned towards them. "I'm heading back to my room. We have an early game," Jay said. "Let's get some rest and win this whole tournament."

"Aye, Aye, Captain," Tanner said.

With that, everyone went off to their own rooms, and got a good night's sleep.

That weekend, they did exactly what their captain told them to do—they won every game they played, and won the tournament. But more importantly, there was a major shift happening on the Renegades. Jay was starting to earn the respect of his teammates, and Brendan was becoming the odd man out.

CHAPTER 35

Jay's phone buzzed, but he didn't know where it was coming from. He unpacked his bag from Regina, and threw most of his clothes in small piles around his room. As he searched, his phone buzzed again to remind him of the text message. He found his phone under a black t-shirt on the floor, and looked at the screen. The text was from Ava.

Hey!! Are you home yet?

Jay typed back: *Hey!!! I got home about a half hour ago.*

He left the phone on his bed and threw some clothes into his hamper while he waited for a reply. His phone buzzed again.

I want to hear all about your tournament. Want to come over?

Jay was tired, but he didn't text Ava all weekend. He was too busy playing hockey and actually hanging out with his teammates. That weekend was the first time in a while that he hadn't hung out with Ava. He had so much to tell her.

Jay grabbed the medal he won from the tournament, put it in his front pocket, and went to his mom's room.

"Mom, can I go to Ava's?" Jay asked.

Jay's mom was also unpacking her bag from the weekend. She looked tired.

"Are you sure you want to? It's Sunday night and you had a busy weekend. Plus, you'll see her tomorrow," his mom said.

"I'll just go for a bit. I want to show her my medal."

"Just for a bit then," his mom said, and threw one of her balled-up pairs of socks at him.

Jay caught them before they hit him. "Gross! I don't want to touch your smelly socks," he said, and threw them right back at her.

His mom wasn't prepared for a return throw, and they hit her right in the forehead. She had an immediate look of surprise on her face. "Did you just throw socks at my head?"

"I'm sorry, I didn't mean to!" Jay said. He felt bad, but they couldn't have hurt. They were just socks after all.

His mom snorted and started to laugh, and then Jay started to laugh.

"You better get out of here before a sock war starts!" his mom said holding up another pair of socks—ready to fire.

"I'm going, I'm going," Jay said, and he put his arms over his head, and ran out the door. The pair of socks hit him in the back just as he got into the hallway. He laughed again, but kept on going down the stairs. When he got to the back door, he texted Ava to let her know he was on his way.

Even though it was in the middle of January, Jay decided it took too much effort to put on his winter jacket. So, he put on his shoes, and ran down the street to Ava's house. When he got to their front door, he rang the doorbell. As he stood there, he started shivering. He knew it was cold, but he didn't think it was that cold. Finally, Ava answered the door.

"What are you doing?" Ava said, greeting him. "It's minus thirty-five outside. Get in here."

"It's a lot colder than I thought," Jay said shaking his arms when he got inside.

"It's called a jacket. You're supposed to wear one in winter," Ava said teasingly.

"Jacket? Never heard of it."

"You're so stupid," Ava said. "I should have left you out there."

"Ouch," Jay said. "Since you're being so mean...I would leave...but it's too cold to go back out there."

"I'm sorry, I didn't mean it. Better?" Ava said jokingly.

"Much better," Jay said.

They both walked to the kitchen and Mrs. Berwin was in there. "Hi, Mrs. Berwin," Jay said.

"Hi, Jay," Mrs. Berwin said. She took one look at Jay who was still shivering. "It's cold out there, isn't it?"

"Yeah, and this dumb-dumb didn't wear a jacket," Ava said, already forgetting her apology.

"Hey, Ava, be nice," Mrs. Berwin said. "What are you trying to do freeze out there? Sheesh. Would you like some hot chocolate?"

Jay laughed. "I would love some," Jay said.

Mrs. Berwin put some water to boil and Jay and Ava sat down at the table.

"So, how was Regina?" Ava asked.

"It was really good. We never lost a game and we won the whole tournament," Jay said.

"Congratulations, Jay," Mrs. Berwin said.

"Wow, nice work," Ava said. "Score any goals?"

"I got seven goals and six assists," Jay replied.

"Holy, that's great!" Ava said.

"I also have a sort of funny story to tell you about Brendan," Jay said. He looked at Mrs. Berwin who was pouring hot water into two mugs. "But I will tell you later."

"Is it something bad and that's why you can't tell her now?" Mrs. Berwin said filling the second mug. Moms always seem to know everything.

"It's not that bad," Jay said. "I can tell it now."

He then told Ava and her mom the story about the laxative as they sat around the table and drank their hot chocolate. But he did leave out the part about the vaping. He didn't know if he should tell Coach Steven or someone else about that yet.

"I don't know what is going on with that boy," Mrs. Berwin said. "He used to be a nice kid, but he seems to get worse and worse as he gets older. I hope he smartens up."

"I'm so happy you stood up for yourself," Ava said. "I wish I could have seen his face when you shoved that donut in his mouth. That would have been priceless."

"I must admit it felt good. But I'm a bit worried at what he will do to me. He's not someone that would let something like that go," Jay said.

"Hopefully his dad will stop him from doing anything else terrible," Ava said. "But, let's change the subject. I actually have some exciting news. Tyler got asked to be an affiliate for the Saskatoon Contacts. Which means if he plays well, there's a good chance he will play with them next year."

"That' so awesome!" Jay said. He was super happy for Tyler.

"And there's more. He will probably be showing up to your morning skates before school. I hope you don't mind," Ava said, and took a sip of her hot chocolate.

"Mind? Why would I mind. I would love for him to come out there. I would learn so much more from him," Jay said.

"I think Tyler's looking to learn from you," Mrs. Berwin said smiling.

Jay didn't know what to say to that. He thought she was joking at first, but he could tell she wasn't. Jay still didn't quite understand how good he actually was.

When they finished their hot chocolate, Ava showed Jay some of the homework he missed on Friday afternoon. He knew he wouldn't be able to finish it that night, but he would try to finish it in the morning before school—but after his morning skate, of course.

"Oh, yeah, I have something for you," Jay said to Ava while he finished putting on his shoes. He stood up, and pulled the medal he won from the tournament out of his pocket. "This is my first hockey medal and I want you to have it," Jay said. He didn't know why but he felt awkward saying it.

"I can't take that," Ava said.

"Yes, you can. I wouldn't have won it without you."

"What do you mean? I don't play hockey."

"Without you being my friend, I probably would have moved schools, or went back to Calgary, and never played hockey…we're a team after all," Jay said.

Ava took the medal and gave Jay a hug. "We sure are," she said smiling.

Jay ran back home feeling like everything was falling into place.

CHAPTER 36

Jay's team went on a huge ten game winning streak after he was named the new captain. Going into the final two months of the season, the Renegades had a good shot at winning cities, and making it far into Provincials. But the more they won, and the better they were getting, Brendan was making it more difficult for the team to win.

Brendan would no longer pass the puck to anyone, and he started to get several penalties each game. Everything made him angry and he showed zero discipline on the ice—it's like he wanted them to lose. Coach Steven had trouble controlling his own son. Benching him never seemed to work, and Coach didn't know what to do. Was he supposed to kick his own son off the team?

As captain, Jay tried to talk to Brendan, but it almost always led to Brendan threatening Jay in some way. It then became Jay's role to try and hold the rest of the team together while they were forced to play shorthanded. Jay had to step up his game even more, and he must have set some sort of record with all the shorthanded goals that he was scoring.

Not only was Brendan making things difficult for the Renegades, Jay started to take a beating as Captain. That "C" really did put a target on his chest. Even though it was still non-contact at his age, that didn't stop other teams from playing dirty and trying to take Jay out of the game. This started to happen more and more once Jay's team started to play the two-game playdowns to see who would move forward in Provincials. These two-game playdowns counted goals for and against, and so each team was trying to score as many goals as possible and they would do anything to stop the other team from scoring too many.

In the first game in a series against the Saskatoon Bobcats, near the end of the second period, the Renegades were winning 9-3. Jay was digging hard in the corner in their end, when a big defenseman came from in front of the net and cross-checked Jay from behind into the boards. When Jay got hit, the entire arena went silent. A check like that could have caused a serious injury. Luckily, Jay didn't end up getting hurt. He got up slowly, just to be careful, and skated off without any sign that he was hurt at all. The player that hit him, received a game-misconduct, which meant he was out for the rest of the game. One of their players also had to serve a five-minute major penalty.

Jay wasn't hurt by that check, but it did make him angry. It made him play even harder. He wasn't going to get revenge by hurting anyone, instead he was going to make them pay on the scoreboard. Jay's next shift out, he made the score 10-3.

Everyone watching couldn't believe how tough this kid was. He was out there taking a beating, and it looked liked nothing could stop him. Not only that, it only seemed to make him stronger and better. The Renegades ended up winning that game 11-4.

Jay walked out of the dressing room, and Uncle Dylan was waiting for him. "What a game," Uncle Dylan said, and he patted Jay on the shoulder.

"Thanks, Unc."

They started walking towards the parking lot doors.

"Man, you got crushed from behind. That was a dirty hit," Uncle Dylan said. "How you feeling, Neph?"

"Yeah, I'm fine. Didn't hurt at all."

"That's good. But you can't be taking hits like that forever."

"Not much I can do about that," Jay replied. He had to squeeze in between several other parents that were waiting around and talking in front of the other team's dressing room.

"At some point you will have to stand up for yourself, or someone will need to stand up for you," Uncle Dylan continued as they got through the crowd.

"What do you mean?" Jay asked.

"You might have to hit back or someone will have to hit back for you, so they become afraid of you," Uncle Dylan said.

"That's not me though. I hit back on the scoreboard."

"Unfortunately, that's only going to make them take more runs at you."

Jay and his uncle Dylan met up with his mom and grandparents, who also congratulated him, and they all walked out together.

The whole way home, Jay thought about what his uncle said and he had a point. He needed to stick up for himself, or he might get hurt. He knew he couldn't take hits like that forever. But he also didn't want to spend time in the penalty box or get kicked out of a game. Jay didn't know what to do. But someone had to do something. It would only get harder the further they got in Provincial playoffs.

CHAPTER 37

"I wonder what's going on," Ava said to Jay. They were sitting in class right after lunch, and Mr. Young still wasn't back in the classroom. Brendan was also missing.

"Who knows. But the longer Mr. Young takes, the less math we will have to do," Jay said.

Ava laughed. "I like math."

"Boring," Jay said teasing her.

"You're boring," Ava said and glared at Jay.

"Hey, now!"

While Jay and Ava were going back and forth like they normally did, Ryan got up from his desk, and walked over to Jay.

"Did you hear that Brendan got suspended?" Ryan asked.

"Really? Good," Jay said. "But what did he do? He didn't do anything to me for once."

"He got caught vaping in the bathroom," Ryan replied. "Mr. Young caught him."

"What an idiot," Jay said. "Wait, we have our first playoff game tonight against Prince Albert. As much as I hate to say it, I hope he can still play tonight."

"Hasn't he just been getting penalties?" Ava said joining the conversation.

"He's been a bit better since his dad benched him for a full game," Jay told Ava.

"Either way, we need him. I heard PA is tough," Ryan said.

Mr. Young walked into the classroom, and Ryan went back to his desk. Brendan didn't return to class the rest of the day. As much as Jay didn't like Brendan, he felt bad that Brendan was wasting all of his hockey talent. If Coach Steven benched Brendan again, Jay knew that he would have to do everything he could to help the Renegades win.

That night, Jay pushed the dressing room door open, and was greeted by the familiar smell of hockey sweat. That smell no longer bothered him—it was simply the smell of hockey. Brendan was the only one sitting there, and he looked up, and went back to scrolling on his phone.

Jay dropped his bag, and sat down across from Brendan. "I heard you got suspended today for…vaping?"

"It's none of your business, loser," Brendan said without looking up from his phone.

"It is my business. Like it or not but we are teammates. I want to know what's going on with you. All the penalties, vaping, being a jerk to everyone. You used to play hockey. You used to be the best player. What happened?"

"You want to know what happened? You happened!" Brendan said looking at Jay with rage in his eyes. "You came here from wherever, and you're taking everything from me. My school, my team, my C, my dad. Everything."

"I never took anything from you. You threw it away," Jay said. "Don't you understand that we could have the best team in the province if you stopped messing around, stopped vaping, and just played how you can play. Nobody could beat us. Nobody."

Suddenly Chad pushed the door open, and rolled his bag in. Jay and Brendan both went silent.

"What's up, Jay. Brendan," Chad said.

"Hey, Chad," Jay said.

Brendan nodded at Chad and grunted. Jay hoped that Brendan's silence meant that maybe, only maybe, he was thinking about what Jay had said. More players quickly followed after Chad, and they all started to get ready for the game.

The Prince Albert Eagles were a big, strong team. But right from the start, Brendan was playing like a madman out there. He scored the first two goals of the game early on, and Jay wondered if his speech had worked. But then Brendan got a penalty for slashing and one for roughing almost back-to-back within the last ten minutes of the period, and the Eagles tied the game up.

Three minutes into the second period, with the flick of his wrist, and a quick spin, Jay won the faceoff down in the Eagle's zone. He passed the puck back to Tommy on defense, and he took a high wrist-shot that bounced off the goalie's chest. The puck trickled out to Jay who was at the left side of the slot. The goalie panicked and went down, and Jay fired the puck top-shelf over the glove-hand side. With that goal, the Renegades went ahead 3-2.

On Jay's next shift, Jay scored on a breakaway to make the score 4-2. With the way he was playing, the Eagles started to put extra pressure on him. They had one player nearly shadow Jay for the rest of the second period, but he made them pay for it. He was able to draw the shadow away from their position and his linemates were left wide open. Jay notched two assists that period, and that put them up 6-2.

The attempt at shadowing Jay officially ended, when he picked up a loose puck, and he took it all the way back behind his own net. When the shadow tried to follow, Jay skated out, and his shadow chased right behind him. Then Jay circled behind the net again. Jay was only playing around with them. He was showing everyone out there—the crowd, the other coaches, the other players—how ridiculous their strategy was. Once he had enough, he came out from behind the net, and then blasted off as fast as he could. He made everyone out there look like pilons as he skated right by them. He went from end to end, made one quick fake like he was going to shoot, and then cut to his backhand and slid the puck across the ice right past the goalie's skate. No one shadowed Jay for the rest of the game. In fact, it was as if no one even defended him at all.

The Eagle's lost all confidence when their shadow wasn't able to stop Jay, and after that, the Renegades scored three more goals. They won the game 10-3, and Jay finished the game with four goals and two assists.

The next game the Renegades traveled down to Prince Albert to face the Eagles again. The Eagles didn't stand a chance, and the Renegades glided to a 12-5 victory to win the series. It was a rough game filled with penalties, but the refs were able to keep it from getting too out of control.

During the second half of the season, the Renegades were destroying the competition, and most games weren't even close. They were on a hot streak as they moved on to face the Regina Hawks for the Provincial championship.

CHAPTER 38

Jay's eyes shot open the morning of the Saskatoon Renegades' first game against the Regina Hawks. He had a dream that he scored the game winning goal in overtime, and everyone threw off their gloves into the air, and piled on top of him in celebration. The dream felt so real and so awesome that Jay couldn't wait to try and recreate that moment in real life.

Jay went downstairs and his mom was sitting at the kitchen table studying for an exam.

"Good morning, Jay-Jay," his mom said, and she closed one of her books.

"Morning, mom," Jay said.

"You know, you have a big game today, you don't have to be up so early," his mom said.

"Of course I know I have a big game today! I had a dream about it and it woke me up."

"Oh, no. Did you have a nightmare?"

"No! I had the best dream. We won the provincials and I scored the game winning goal," Jay said. "Now I can't wait to get on the ice and make it happen."

Jay's mom smiled. "Look at us, kiddo. Things are much better this year, aren't they? You're about to win provincials and I'm almost done law school."

Jay had often thought about how much better this year was than the year before. "Way better!" Jay replied. He then went to the cupboard, grabbed a bowl, opened a drawer, grabbed a spoon, and then grabbed a box of Cinnamon Toast Crunch from the pantry. Then Jay filled his bowl with cereal.

"Do you think that's a good idea on game day?" his mom asked.

"What this?" Jay said lifting the box of cereal. "What's wrong with it?"

"It's full of sugar," his mom replied. "It's like eating dessert for breakfast."

Jay laughed. "Grampa says that with the amount of brown sugar that I put in my oatmeal, Cinnamon Toast Crunch is the lesser of the evils."

Jay's mom laughed. "He is probably right on that one."

Jay went over to the fridge and grabbed a carton of milk and then poured some in his bowl of cereal. He then put the milk away, carried his bowl and spoon beside his mom, and sat down.

"You ready for your test?" Jay asked, and put a large spoonful of cereal in his mouth.

"I better be…because I won't be doing anymore studying with all that crunching. What are you eating rocks?"

Jay almost spit out some of his cereal at his mom's joke. He tried to apologize but his mouth was still too full.

"Sorry," he managed to say in between bites.

"Don't worry, I'm just teasing you. I'm as ready as I will ever be," she said. "But I'll still study more after your game and tomorrow just to be sure."

Jay was proud of his mom. She worked so hard, and now she was almost all done. "Where's grandma and grandpa?" Jay asked.

"They went to do a bit of shopping and run some errands before your game," Jay's mom replied. "They're very excited, they have been telling everyone. Uncle Dylan's very excited too and he is coming here before your game, then we're all coming to watch."

"Ava and her family are coming too, and I think Mr. Young," Jay said.

"So many people are excited to watch you play, Jay-Jay."

The thought of all those people coming to watch him play

made him nervous, but that nervousness disappeared. Jay knew that all he had to do was do his best, and never stop skating.

Jay finished his cereal and then tried to find something to pass the time. He watched some TV, went in the garage to shoot some pucks, and did a lot of waiting around until it was time to head to the rink.

CHAPTER 39

Jay arrived at the Cosmo Arena, and the Regina Hawks team was getting off the bus in front of him. Jay had to follow their entire team down the long winding path to the rink entrance. He wanted to pass by them, but there was no way to go. Instead, he was forced to follow right behind a tall man with a dark, black beard. The man was carrying a hockey bag and two sticks, and Jay thought it was weird for someone's dad to carry their equipment. But he didn't look old enough to be someone's dad, so Jay thought that maybe it was a coach.

The man held the door open for Jay. "After you, little dude," the man said with a sly smirk on his face. The way he said it, he didn't seem like he was being polite.

Jay gave a nod, and went past him.

Before the game, everyone was all business in the dressing room. There wasn't a lot of joking around. Instead, everyone listened to music, got focused, and tried to get rid of any nervousness. Jay preferred this business-like atmosphere, compared to Brendan calling him loser or trying to make some other lame joke. They were finally behaving like a championship team, and they had two games left to prove it.

When the coaches walked in, someone turned off the music, and the dressing room was silent. "Alright, fellas, this is it," Coach Steven said. "This is what we play for. We play all season to win a championship, and now we're almost there. All you need to do is go out there and play like you did against P.A. We can win this Provincial Championship. I know you can do it, but will you do it? Let that sink in for a moment." Coach Steven paced back and forth and looked at each player, and continued. "Now go out there, play hard, score like you can, get the puck out of our zone, and stay out of the penalty box. It's that simple. Now, helmets on, and let's go!"

The Renegades jumped up, started yelling, and Chad led them all out onto the ice. They were all pumped up, excited, and felt like they were going to win. But that quickly went away when they all saw Number Four—the captain of the Regina Hawks.

As the Renegades circled their half of the ice to start their warm-up, one by one, they observed the Regina captain skating around the ice like he was in the NHL. He took a slapshot that rang off the crossbar. Then circled, picked up the puck, went in on his backhand and put the puck bar-down. *Who is this guy?* Jay thought. *He's going to score thirty goals.*

Jay wasn't the only one that noticed. While they were in the lineup for the horseshoe, they all stared in amazement.

"We're toast," Ryan said.

"Can we just forfeit now," Kyle said.

"Look it at his stick…he can reach right across the ice with that thing," Mike added.

All the Renegades seemed to have lost their confidence. But Jay reminded himself of all those times he played with Ava's older brother, and he was up for the challenge. He realized there was one way that he could beat Number Four, and that was by getting under his skin. Jay wasn't going to be dirty, but he was going to be the "gnat" that he was the first time he played with the older kids. He was going to do whatever it took to not make it easy on that Number Four, and hoped his team would follow his lead.

When they lined up for the opening faceoff, Jay was relieved to see that their captain was a defenceman. *He won't be able to score thirty goals from back there,* Jay thought. *But it will be tough to score on him when he's out there.*

Jay won the faceoff back to his defenceman, and he put it up the boards. It bounced up to their captain, and with long powerful strides, he skated right by two Renegades into the Renegade zone. Jay was closing in, and what he saw caught him off guard. In a split second, he saw that Number Four had a black beard under his mask, and he was skating in with a smirk on his face. It was the same guy that held the door open for Jay before the game. It wasn't a coach after all.

Before Jay could close the gap, their captain took a quick slapshot, and the puck flew like a rocket to the top corner of the Renegade's net. The Regina Hawks were already up 1-0 on the first shift of the game.

Maybe he will score those thirty goals, Jay thought. Jay had a game plan, but it already failed. He knew that he couldn't give their captain any open ice at all. He had to be on him like glue. He had to shadow him, like other teams tried to do to Jay in the past.

Brendan had another strategy. In the middle of the first period, Regina was up 2-0. Their captain carried it over the blueline, and Brendan tripped him completely on purpose. This took Brendan off the ice, and their captain was still out there for the power play. Brendan's strategy would never work. Regina scored on a rebound from another rocket-like slapshot by their captain. Chad didn't even see the puck, but it bounced right off his pad to an open Regina player, and they put it in the net to make it 3-0. Their captain already had two goals and one assist.

It was still only the first period, but Jay noticed that everyone on his bench look defeated—even the coaches. He knew that he needed to do something soon to make sure the game didn't get too far away from them.

On Jay's next shift, their captain was on the ice too—it seemed like he was always out there. The Renegades struggled to get the puck out of their zone, and they kept passing it blindly up the boards to their defencemen, and they kept peppering Chad with hard shots. Matt had the puck in the corner, and he panicked again, and passed it up the boards. Jay saw what was going to happen, and he broke towards their captain who got the puck, and wound up for another slapshot. Jay skated as fast as he could and stepped in front of him. Everyone in the arena gasped. Jay's mom, grandma, and Ava covered their eyes. Jay closed his eyes in anticipation. Their captain slapped the puck and it hit Jay like a shotgun right in the knee, and bounced to center ice. Jay was still flying, and he raced to get the puck. He scooped it up well before anyone else, and he was on a breakaway. He skated in on the Regina goalie, and he deked to the left, and made a hard cut to the right, and put the puck through the goalie's five-hole as he slid across.

Jay raised his arms, and as he cut to the corner, he saw his Uncle Dylan and grandpa pounding the glass like crazy with huge smiles on their faces. That made him smile, too. Mike, Tanner, Matt, and Tommy skated over and celebrated with him, and he could tell he gave them some hope again. Jay showed everyone out there that with a little sacrifice, winning was still possible. But for him, that hope faded. Jay reached down at his knee to adjust his shinpad, and he felt that the knee on his shinpad was shattered. Without a shinpad, he wouldn't be able to play—at least he shouldn't play.

Back on the bench, Jay reached under his pant leg, and rolled his sock down. As soon as he did that, many little pieces of plastic fell on the ground.

"Coach, my shinpad's busted," Jay said.

"What?" Coach Steven said.

"Look," Jay said, and pointed to the shattered plastic on his shinpad.

"That's not good," Coach Steven said. "How's the knee?"

"It's fine. I didn't feel a thing. But there's nothing left to protect it."

"Anyone have an extra shinpad kicking around?" Coach Steven asked jokingly.

As he was trying to figure something out, the crowd cheered.

Regina had gone up 4-1.

"What happened?" Coach Steven yelled out.

"We gave up a two on one...nice pass and they scored," Coach Brian said.

"Unbelievable," Coach Steven said. "We need to get Jay back out there."

"What if we bundle up another sock on the front of my knee and tape it in place. I'll be fine," Jay said.

"It's too risky," Coach Steven said shaking his head.

"I won't block any shots," Jay insisted.

"I'll call someone to go look in lost and found, or something," Coach Steven said. He looked stressed.

In that time, Jay had already missed two shifts, but the Renegades managed to keep Regina from scoring. Then, with less than two minutes left in the period, Brendan got a slashing penalty.

"You got to be kidding me," Coach Steven shouted at Brendan, with his arms up in the air.

Then he got an idea. Coach Steven went to the penalty box, and got Brendan to take off his shinpad. With a lot of reluctance, Brendan finally did, and handed it over the glass. Jay was able to swap shinpads quickly, and they put him out for the penalty kill.

Brendan's shinpad was bigger than his, and he tried to adjust it as he stepped onto the ice for the faceoff. Jay was playing the biggest game of his life, against the toughest opponent, and things were not getting any easier.

Jay won the faceoff, and Tommy fired it blindly around the boards.

"Keep it away from him!" Coach Brian hollered.

Jay saw what was going to happen again, and he got on their captain right away, and chipped the puck past him. With his long reach, their captain was able to pick up the puck again, but Jay stayed on him, and forced him to pass the puck. Ryan was able to get a stick on the puck, and he fired it down the ice.

Jay raced their captain for the puck, and Jay proved he was faster. He picked up the puck, carried it around the boards, but he felt his pad shift off of his knee, so he dumped the puck back in and headed to the bench. There was a little over a minute left in the penalty, and twenty seconds left in the period. Jay sat on the bench and tried to realign Brendan's shinpad. He knew that he couldn't play the game swapping shinpads back and forth. They needed to figure something else out.

The buzzer went, and the Renegades headed off the ice for the first intermission. When they got to the dressing room, they all looked exhausted. Everyone was covered in sweat.

"Give me back my shinpad, loser," Brendan said.

Jay looked at Brendan. "You know what? You need to start being a team player or we will never win this game. I'm going to give you back your shinpad, but you need to stay out of the box, and start playing hockey. I won't be able to play, so it's up to you now."

Everyone sat in silence. They hated to see their captain have to sit out. Eventually, all three coaches entered, and Coach Steven was looking at his phone. "I have some good news," Coach Steven said to Jay. "Tyler went home to get his old shinpads. We should be able to get you some by the middle of the second period. Until then, let's try and build you a shin pad. As for everyone else, you saw what your captain did out there. Each one of you will have to dig deep and make some sacrifices of your own. Number four is killing us. We need to stay on him, and try to get some goals when he's not out there. Keep working hard, and we can stay in this. Remember that it's a two-game total of goals for and against, so it doesn't matter much if we lose today, it matters how much we lose by."

Coach Steven and Coach Brian went over to Jay. Coach Brian grabbed his shattered shinpad, and Coach Steven gave him a folded, black hockey sock, and shoved it where the plastic knee would be. Coach Brian put sock tape over the sock in a bunch of different directions.

"It's not pretty, but it will be better than nothing to start the period," Coach Brian said, and he handed the shinpad to Jay.

"Let's hope Tyler gets here quick," Coach Steven said. "And no blocking any shots. Understood?"

"Understood," Jay said.

Jay wasn't worried about playing with a busted shinpad. He never used any equipment when he played on the outdoor rink. He just needed to remember to stay away from any hard slapshots—especially their captain's slapshot.

Jay looked around at his exhausted teammates, and knew he had to keep leading by example. There were two periods left, and Jay was ready to give it his all.

CHAPTER 40

The Renegades came out for the second period showing that they would not be outworked. They battled hard for the puck, and they didn't give the Regina captain any open ice. For the most part, they were able to gain some confidence and come together as a team. Unfortunately, the Renegades were already down 4-1, and they had to dig themselves out of a hole.

Jay continued to work hard out there, but with his broken shinpad, he wasn't able to get in front of shots, or put himself where he needed to be. He had to move out of the way of their captain's slapshots, and this gave the Hawks good chances to score. His broken equipment was still holding him back. But eight minutes into the period, Tyler showed up with a pair of shinpads. Jay made the swap, and instantly felt invincible.

His very next shift, he was getting in front of shots once again, and he almost tipped a shot into the other team's net. The Renegades continued to keep the Hawks from scoring, but the Renegades couldn't put the puck in the net. Coach Steven decided there was only one thing they could do to try and make a comeback.

"Brendan and Jay," Coach Steven said back on the bench. "I am putting you on a line together. It's our only chance to get back in this game. Do you think you can work together?"

"Yes, coach," Jay said instantly.

"Brendan?" Coach Steven said.

"Whatever," Brendan answered.

"Alright, Brendan you'll play centre, Jay you'll take right, and

Mike you'll be left on their line," Coach Steven said. He was willing to take the risk, and he hoped that his son would finally be the teammate he knew he could be.

After a few shifts together, it paid off. Jay picked up a loose puck in the Regina zone, saw Brendan in the slot, and passed the puck right on his tape. Brendan put it top corner to make the game 4-2. Following that goal, the Renegade's bench and all their fans in the stands came back to life.

"Nice goal, son," Coach Steven said as they got back to the bench. "And nice pass, Jay."

Brendan never thanked Jay for that pass, but that didn't matter. Getting the goal was enough.

The next few times out, Brendan carried the puck, and still wouldn't pass to Jay. Brendan may have stopped getting penalties, but it was clear that he was a one-man-show. This was something that the other team noticed as well. When the Regina captain was out there, he started to go directly at Brendan, and knocked him off the puck each time. While that was happening, Jay and Mike were wide open, and they called several times for the puck, but Brendan would never pass.

"Pass the puck!" Coach Steven yelled, as their line got back to the bench.

Brendan smirked. Even though they had a chance to get back in the game, he was not willing to play as a team.

Jay was frustrated, but he didn't say anything. He realized a long time ago that he couldn't make Brendan change his mind. No one could.

But being on Brendan's line was still the right move. Jay was able to be right on the Regina captain every time he had the puck, and Jay kept him from getting any good scoring chances. Jay was able to frustrate their captain, and near the end of the second period, their captain hit Jay hard into the boards. Jay's head hit the edge where the glass and boards meet, and he crumpled to the ice. He had never been hit that hard before. He slowly got back up, but, when he looked around, everything had a green tinge to it. He also couldn't hear anything. Everything was muffled. He saw Coach Brian doing the run-run-slide that coaches have to do to get to where they want to go on the ice. Jay could see that his coach was saying something, but he couldn't make out the words.

Jay continued to the bench with Coach Brian by his side. As he sat down, sound came roaring back, but his ears were ringing.

"Jay, are you all right?" Coach Brian said, and leaned over him.

Coach Steven also came over to check on him.

"Yeah, I think I'm fine," Jay said.

"Are you sure?" Coach Steven asked.

"I'm sure."

"You are one tough kid," Coach Steven said, and patted Jay on the shoulder pad.

Jay never told his coach that he couldn't hear anything, that his ears were ringing, and that everything looked green.

Jay didn't know it then, but he had a concussion.

Brendan came back to the bench and sat down beside Jay. "I'll make that ogre pay next shift," Brendan said.

Jay was surprised. He looked over at Brendan. "The only way we can really make him pay is by beating them on the scoreboard," Jay said.

"Fine, let's do it then," Brendan said, and tapped Jay on his left shinpad with his stick.

Jay looked at Brendan in disbelief. "Let's do it then."

Their next shift out, Brendan lost the faceoff in the Hawk's end, and the puck went back to Number Four. Jay rushed after him as he went behind the net, but Brendan cut him off, knocked the puck off his stick, and managed to chip it to Jay. Brendan circled back to the left side of the slot, and Jay made a nice move around the other defenseman. Jay saw that Brendan was open, and he slid the puck over, and Brendan slapped a one-timer into the open net.

The score was now 4-3.

Brendan skated over to Jay. "Nice pass," Brendan said, and tapped him on the shinpad again.

They went back to centre ice for the faceoff.

It was now a one-goal game, but that's not the most important thing that happened. For the first time, Brendan and Jay became a team.

CHAPTER 41

In the dressing room during the second intermission, the energy shifted. Many noticed Brendan tap Jay on the shinpad for the first time. With both of them leading the team, the Regina Hawks didn't stand a chance. They may have been down by one goal, but the Renegades knew they were a championship team.

"Alright, gentleman," Coach Steven began right before they headed out to the ice. "When we go out there, we will have twenty minutes to tie this game up and get the lead. I am proud of all of you. Chad, you're standing on your head out there. You're a big reason we are still in this. Keep up the good work. Everyone else, you're all playing your hearts out. And our captain has been blocking shots, getting his head pounded in, and he's still getting out there to make sure we have a shot at winning this. Let's all do the same for him. We have a real chance. With Jay and Brendan working together, that big-shot Regina captain won't be able to be everywhere. So, let's get out there, tie it up, and show everyone we are the champions."

The Renegades were now fired up for the third period. They all got up at once and many shouted. "LET'S GO!"

Jay's line was due up third that period, and Brendan and Jay talked strategy.

"Hey, Captain," Brendan said. "We got this. That number four can't be on both of us. When you have the puck, I'll be open. When I have the puck, you get open. Let's win this."

Jay looked at Brendan like he was seeing him for the first time, and that familiar look of hatred on Brendan's face was gone.

Jay felt a sense of relief that he hadn't felt since he moved to Saskatoon. "Let's win this," Jay said.

Jay and Brendan weren't the only ones planning to win. Everyone on the Renegades played a role out there. On the second shift of the period, Ryan battled in front of the net, and was able to tie the game on a deflection.

The momentum continued on the Renegades side. Chad was like a brick wall and he made save after save. The Renegades refused to let the Hawks take the lead. Jay and Brendan's strategy worked, and they had awesome chances, but their goalie was also standing on his head. On both sides of the ice, everyone seemed to have been giving it their all. It was exciting playoff hockey.

In the last five minutes of the game, it was still tied 4-4. On another nice pass from Jay, right between Number Four's long stick, Brendan skated in, and put the puck off the post. Everyone on the Renegades' bench jumped up because they thought it was in, but the play continued.

After his shift, Jay sat on the bench, squirted water in his mouth, and looked up at the clock. There was only four minutes left in the game. He knew that he had to score. He knew he was going to score. He wasn't going to let his team down. Jay stood up and leaned against the boards ready for his next shift, which would be his last of the game.

With a minute and a half left, Jay's line got on the ice. Brendan won the faceoff in their own zone, but they couldn't get it out. The Regina captain walked in with the puck and fired a hard shot, but Chad made the save with his blocker. The puck went into the corner, and this time Mike was able to get the puck out, and he passed it to Brendan in the neutral zone. Brendan beat the first defenseman and it was a two-on-one. It was Brendan and Jay against the Hawk's captain, with less than a minute left in the game.

The Brendan of old would have tried to take the puck to the net and get a shot off. The Brendan of old, would have never passed to Jay. Brendan looked as if he was going to take the shot from the top of the circle, and Number Four cheated a bit and closed the gap on Brendan. But Brendan pulled the puck back, and sent a beautiful saucer pass that landed right on Jay's stick. The Hawk's captain tried to recover, but Jay sped toward the net on his own.

Jay—the kid that learned how to skate the year before— faked the shot, cut the other way to his backhand, and slid the puck through the five-hole once again. The Renegades went ahead 5-4 with nine seconds left on the clock.

Jay raised his arms in an explosion of happiness. Brendan was the first one to skate over, and he wrapped his arms around Jay. Then all of his linemates surrounded them. In that moment, they became a united team.

Then after a quick faceoff, and the buzzer, their whole team jumped out onto the ice. The Renegades never gave up, and they worked together to make an unbelievable comeback. Jay Noble led by example. And with one more win, they could be the champions they deserved to be.

CHAPTER 42

The day before the final provincial game, Jay and Ava were working on their science project in class, when Brendan came walking over to their desks. Both of his hands were in fists.

"Heads up, Jay," Ava said and lifted her chin in Brendan's direction.

Brendan stood over them, and suddenly lifted his right fist in front of him. Jay flinched.

"Noble, you and I are going to destroy Regina tomorrow. Let's do what we did in the third period last game," Brendan said.

Jay hesitated for a moment, looked up at Brendan, and then lightly pounded Brendan's knuckle. "Let's do it."

Mr. Young watched what was going on and walked over to them. "Is everything all good over here?"

"All good," Brendan said. "Jay and I are going to win provincials tomorrow."

"I heard you had an excellent game last weekend. I believe you boys will do it. Teamwork goes a long way, doesn't it?" Mr. Young said.

The boys smiled. But before they could say anything, Mr. Young continued. "Brendan you should probably get back to your partner, so Jay and Ava can continue their teamwork on this project."

Brendan nodded, and he went back to his desk.

"Umm, did I miss something," Ava said. "Are you two besties now?"

"I wouldn't go that far, but after last game, we are teammates now…but you never know, we may become besties someday," Jay said.

"There is no way he is stealing you from me," Ava said. "But I did tell you at the start of the season you should have given him a hug. So much drama could have been avoided."

"You did say that, didn't you?" Jay said remembering the day after he found out he made the team.

"I sure did. And I'm always right," Ava said and smiled.

"That you are. Why do you think I'm your partner for this science project…easy marks for me."

"Oh, are you saying you're only partners with me so you can get easy marks?"

"That and for other reasons."

"What kind of other reasons?" Ava asked, and wrote some things in her binder.

"Well, the main reason is that you are my best friend. It's just a bonus you are super smart," Jay said.

"That means you should always listen to me. I think I should call Brendan back over here and you can give him that hug right now."

"He sort of gave me a hug last game. But maybe I'll give him a hug tomorrow on the ice when we win provincials. That way it won't be too weird," Jay said.

Ava laughed. "Maybe I'll give *you* a hug when you win provincials. I wish I could come out to Regina tomorrow."

"You're always looking for an excuse to hug me," Jay said teasingly.

"Is that a bad thing?"

"Not at all," Jay said, and they both smiled at each other.

CHAPTER 43

On the bus ride down to Regina, the atmosphere was light, loose, and calm. Jay sat beside Mike, and right across the aisle was Brendan and Ryan. There wasn't any bullying or separation—all of them talked about winning. Going into that final game, the Renegades were banded together.

In the dressing room, Brendan sat beside Jay for the first time. With that simple act of peace, the entire squad was fired up.

But that wasn't all. This time around, to their advantage, they also knew what to expect. They knew the big, Regina captain would be out there, but they knew how to stop him. If they played the way they did at the end of last game, they would win the provincial championship. That's the attitude all of them had. That's the attitude they carried with them onto the ice.

Brendan skated around the centre faceoff circle and made his way over to Jay. "Alright, Noble," Brendan said punching Jay on the shoulder pad. "Let's have some fun."

Jay grinned. "Let's have some fun," he said tapping Brendan on the shinpad with his stick. They were both ready to show everyone what they could do.

Jay looked over at the Regina Captain on defence. *You don't stand a chance*, Jay thought. It was the last game of the year, but Jay felt like they were just getting started.

Brendan won the opening faceoff, and the defenceman made a quick pass up to Mike. He took it over the red line and fired the puck into the Hawks zone. Jay blazed down the ice like a bullet and beat Number Four to the puck. Jay skated around the net and made a centering pass right to Brendan, and he blasted the puck to the back of the net.

Jay and Mike skated over to Brendan and they both hugged him in celebration. It felt weird for Jay to hug Brendan, but it also felt right. Watch any NHL game, and that's what teammates do when they score big goals. And it was a big goal. This time, on the first rush of the game, the Renegades were up 1-0. After that first goal, they couldn't be stopped.

Jay and Brendan were too good when they worked together. Once they became the linemates everyone knew they could be, they truly became unbeatable.

But the rest of the Renegades also played their part. Everyone worked hard, kept the pressure on in the Hawk's zone, and played solid defense. Chad had another unbelievable game and continued to be a brick wall in net.

Number Four put the Regina Hawks on the board halfway through the first, but when the period ended, the Renegades were already up 3-1. The Hawks wouldn't be able to score another goal.

The Renegades went on to beat the Regina Hawks 7-1. Jay scored three goals and got an assist, and Brendan got two goals and two assists. That kind of talent on the same team doesn't come around too often, and they were a lot of fun to watch.

When the buzzer went at the end of the game, sticks were dropped, and gloves were thrown off. The Renegades all ended up in one happy pile on the ice. Jay had never experienced anything like that before. It was a great feeling.

Once they finished celebrating, they lined up and shook hands with the other team. As they shook hands, Jay noticed many player's faces from the Regina Hawks were puffy from crying— including their six-foot-tall captain. Jay thought it was awkward seeing a grown man cry, but he had to remind himself that kid was only twelve-years-old—just like he was. Jay had been through a lot, but he didn't know what it was like to lose a championship game.

After they finished shaking hands, both teams lined up on their blueline. The player of the game for the Regina Hawks was announced, and it was no surprise that it was their captain. He skated over to the penalty box, shook hands with a man wearing a blue suit, and received the player of the game plaque. Jay could tell there wasn't much joy for their captain as he skated over to get his award.

Then, the player of the game for the Saskatoon Renegades was announced. When Jay Noble's name was called, he was happy, but he felt that anyone on his team deserved it. Jay skated over to the penalty box, shook hands with the man that handed him the plaque. His teammates slapped their sticks so hard on the ice and for so long, he thought they would never stop.

"You are the most talented and hardest working player I have ever seen," the man with the blue suit said. "And I mean that."

"Thanks," Jay said, and he skated back to his spot.

The Renegades watched as the Hawks were given their silver medals. Finally, the Saskatoon Renegades were presented with their gold medals. One by one, a medal was placed around their neck. It was all so formal, and Jay had never experienced anything like it. But when that medal was placed around his neck, he knew that he wanted to win more in the future.

Once the last medal went to Chad, the Renegades were officially the Under-13 A Provincial Champions. They were not only the best team in Saskatoon, they were the best team in the province.

Jay Noble led his team to become provincial champions, won the player of the game, and became the only first-time hockey player to ever do that. Jay's first season playing hockey was truly a remarkable one.

As far as Jay was concerned, he was just a kid that wanted to play hockey, and he played as best as he could.

Back in the dressing room, the Renegades joked, laughed, and talked about all the best parts of the game. They were all happy and they were all having fun.

The coaches walked in, and Coach Steven got them all to quiet down.

"When I look around this room," Coach Steven said. "I have never seen such an amazing group of players. I am proud of each and every one of you. And you should all be proud of yourselves. This team is something special. There were some ups and downs, but you all battled this entire season. You never gave up, and most of all, you came together as a team. That's what champions do. And, you are all champions now. Never forget that. Now enjoy it!"

The Renegades all hollered and cheered after their coach's speech. Jay sat there and looked around the room. This is where he was meant to be. This is where he belonged.

When Jay got on the bus for the long ride back home to Saskatoon, he checked his phone, and he had two messages.

The first one was from his Uncle Dylan: *Congratulations, Neph! So proud of you!!!*

The second one was from Ava: *I guess I owe you a hug when you get home. See you soon!!*

Jay smiled, and read the messages again. He couldn't have imagined not moving to Saskatoon. It was home, and he couldn't wait to get back.

CHAPTER 44

It had only been a week after Provincials before Coach Steven called Jay's mom with some incredible news. A sports writer for the Star Phoenix wanted to do a story on Jay. This writer had heard from someone that the captain of the U13 A Provincial Champions was a kid that not only was playing hockey for the first time, but had learned how to skate just over a year before. The sports writer thought it was a fascinating story and wanted to interview Jay about how he was able to get so good, so fast. He wanted to know his secret. Jay was excited and his mom said that he could do the interview.

Jay couldn't wait to read the article when it ran in the paper a few days later. He woke up before his alarm (which was still set at 6:03 a.m.), and snuck out of his bedroom, and waited in the living room for the newspaper to get delivered. Once he heard the metal mailbox lid shut, he slowly unbolted the front door, and slipped the newspaper out of the mailbox without making a sound. As he slowly worked on closing the front door, his grandpa reached down and grabbed Jay's shoulders. "What are you doing!" his grandpa said.

Jay nearly jumped out of his socks. "Grandpa! You almost scared my legs off."

Jay's grandpa chuckled. "I had a feeling you would be sneaking to get the newspaper as soon as it was dropped off."

"Do you want to read it with me, grandpa?" Jay asked.

"I sure would. Let's go to the kitchen so I can make some coffee."

They headed to the kitchen and Jay tore through the paper to get to the sports section. There, on the front page was the headline *Never Stop Skating* with a picture of Jay leaning on his hockey stick with a giant smile on his face.

Jay was about to start reading, when his mom and grandma both came into the kitchen.

"What's with all the noise this morning?" Jay's mom said, and yawned.

Jay held up the newspaper so they could see the picture of him. "It's here!" Jay said. "Grandpa, can you read it for all of us? You have a good announcer's voice."

"Sure, little buddy," Jay's grandpa said and he reached for the paper.

"And now, for the article, Never Stop Skating!" Jay's grandpa said in a booming announcers voice.

Jay laughed.

"Okay, dad," Jay's mom said. "Are you trying to wake the neighbours?"

"Tough crowd," Jay's grandpa said. "Here we go."

Jay's grandpa started reading the following article:

Never Stop Skating
A Twelve-Year-Old's Secret to Overcoming Challenges
By Kevin Kennedy
of The StarPhoenix

Imagine winning the Under-13 Tier A Provincial Championship. Now imagine being the captain and leading scorer of that championship team. Now imagine that only a year ago, you never played hockey before, and you didn't know how to skate. Imagine moving to a new city. Imagine getting picked on and bullied every day—not only from other kids your age, but also your teacher. Now imagine not letting any of that stop you. That's the incredible story of twelve-year-old Jay Noble of the Saskatoon Renegades.

I had the wonderful opportunity to meet this young man, and let me tell you, his positive attitude is contagious. It is hard to imagine that anyone would want to pick on him. It is hard to imagine that someone who is so dedicated to hockey, only started playing the sport this season.

I talked with his mom, his coaches, and they all say the same thing, they are all amazed at this young man. Steven Walker, the head coach of the U13 A Saskatoon Renegades, said that he had never seen someone with such natural skating ability. "He makes being on the ice look so effortless. He can change speeds, change directions, stop and start again in an instant. He is not only fun to watch out there, he's such a great kid to coach. He works hard, always wants to learn more, and leads by example. He made my job very easy. He has a very bright future ahead of him," Coach Steven Walker said.

When I asked Jay about his experience in Saskatoon so far, he said that he was very lonely at first. All the other boys in his class played hockey, and not having played before, he was left out. When he first played at recess there was an incident with another boy, and this led to a year of misery for Jay. "I had no friends, and they were always blaming me for things I didn't do. It got to the point where my teacher even hated me," Jay said. When asked how he got through it, he said he knew he wanted to play hockey, so that's what he decided to focus on. Jay set his alarm for 6:03 a.m. and went out every single morning that winter. He said he worked hard every day, and one of the teachers at the school saw him out there one morning, and said he should try out for a hockey team the following year.

Incredibly, after that teacher's suggestion, Jay suited up for the first time this season, and made the A team. "He honestly came out of nowhere," Steven Walker said. "And a player like Jay, only comes around once in a lifetime. I'm lucky that I got to coach him."

To add another dimension to this incredible story, Steven Walker's own son was one of the kids that bullied Jay. "I'm not proud of the way my son acted, but I think a lot of it was jealousy. My son didn't know how to deal with seeing someone so talented. Jay and Brendan have both come a long way this season, and I'm proud of both of them."

Jay, who is mature for his age, said this about being bullied, "It was a horrible experience, but as bad as it was, I'm glad I went through it. Knowing that I can overcome something like that, tells me that I can overcome anything."

When asked what his secret is to overcome challenges and be a champion, Jay said, "It's simple, no matter what, never stop skating."

Jay's mom put her arm around Jay and kissed him on the top of his head, "I'm so proud of you, Jay-Jay."

"I'm proud of you too, Jay," his grandma said wiping tears from her eyes.

Jay's grandpa folded the paper and was speechless. Suddenly, Jay ran out of the kitchen, up the stairs, and into his room.

He came back a few moments later hopping on one foot as he was trying to put on a sock on the move. He nearly fell into the wall, but managed to get it on half way. Then, he bent over, lifted his foot, and pulled the sock into place.

"Where do you think you're going?" his mom asked.

"Where else?" Jay replied.

"The rink? But your hockey season is over," his mom said.

Jay gave his mom a strange look, but his grandpa could read Jay's mind. "Never stop skating?" his grandpa said with a smile.

"Never stop skating, grandpa," Jay said.

Jay continued on to the back door, put on his jacket, grabbed his skates, his stick, and headed out towards the rink.

ABOUT THE AUTHOR

Jesse A. Murray is a Canadian author, poet, and high school teacher. He is the author of two novels, a children's chapter book, and five poetry collections. Jesse lives in Saskatoon, Saskatchewan with his wife and two daughters.

Visit jesseamurray.com for more information and current updates on Jesse's future projects.

Connect on socials:
Facebook: @authorjesseamurray
Instagram: @jesse.a.murray
X: @jesseamurray

www.ingramcontent.com/pod-product-compliance
Lightning Source LLC
Chambersburg PA
CBHW031955170626
46807CB00006B/2500